LETTERS FROM THE GINZA SHIHODO STATIONERY SHOP

Kenji Ueda is a Japanese novelist known for blending fantasy with the charm of everyday life. Born in Tokyo in 1969, he made his debut as a writer in 2021 with *Teppan* (The Iron Griddle), the revised version of a work he wrote in 2019 for the 1st Japan Delicious Fiction Award.

LETTERS FROM THE GINZA SHIHODO STATIONERY SHOP

KENJI UEDA
Translated by Emily Balistrieri

MANILLA PRESS

First published in the UK in 2024 by
MANILLA PRESS
An imprint of Bonnier Books UK
5th Floor, HYLO, 103–105 Bunhill Row,
London, EC1Y 8LZ
Owned by Bonnier Books
Sveavägen 56, Stockholm, Sweden

Originally published as 銀座「四宝堂」文房具店 in Japan in 2022
by Shogakukan Inc.

Copyright © by Kenji Ueda, 2022
English Translation Copyright © by Emily Balistrieri, 2024
Translated from Japanese by Emily Balistrieri

All rights reserved. No part of this publication may be reproduced, stored or transmitted in any form by any means, electronic, mechanical, photocopying or otherwise, without the prior written permission of the publisher.

The right of Kenji Ueda to be identified as Author of this work has been asserted by him in accordance with the Copyright, Designs and Patents Act, 1988.

This is a work of fiction. Names, places, events and incidents are either the products of the author's imagination or used fictitiously. Any resemblance to actual persons, living or dead, or actual events is purely coincidental.

A CIP catalogue record for this book is available from the British Library.

ISBN: 978-1-78658-464-9

Also available as an ebook and an audiobook

3 5 7 9 10 8 6 4

Typeset by Envy Design Ltd
Printed and bound in Great Britain by Clays Ltd, Elcograf S.p.A.

Manilla Press is an imprint of Bonnier Books UK

Contents

Fountain Pen	1
Organiser	45
Notebooks	89
Postcards	133
Memo Pads	175

Fountain Pen

The new employee training that had begun on April 1st was finally over. The first two weeks had been classroom study, living at the training centre, but in the third week, we were split into groups and sent to headquarters, factories, sales offices and the laboratory in turn, before giving presentations to our fellow trainees about what we learned from these visits.

With each change of destination, the five-person teams were reorganised, ensuring that we all got the chance to interact with everyone who had joined the company in that batch.

But having to go around with different people every time we went to a new location was utterly stressful for someone shy like me, and I was exhausted.

On top of that, the leadership struggle or, like, one-upmanship among the new employees was rough. HR had told us that 'New employee training is a space for learning, not a place to appraise ability and aptitude,' but in various situations — question time during our field trips for example, or discussions and presentations within our groups — a gap naturally began to open.

Over time and through repetition, a ranking order came into being.

'How did that guy end up here?'

'Prolly someone pulled some strings for him, no?'

The atmosphere had deteriorated to the extent that you

could overhear badmouthing in the break room. In the end, before training was even over, three people had quit.

We're co-workers. We should be helping each other out and getting along. I nearly said it any number of times, but the words wouldn't come out.

That's always how it was with me. I could never speak up about the most important things. And the things I failed to say and therefore wasn't able to convey weighed on me forever.

At this rate, will I manage to survive the sales training coming up after the break? On my way home to an apartment where no one was waiting for me, I was brimming with anxiety despite the fact that I had just received my first pay cheque and had a good stretch of time off.

Rocking along on the subway, I suddenly recalled something one of the older employees had said to us during a training session.

'What are you all going to spend your first pay cheque on? Of course, you can spend it on whatever you like, but if you're able to, I recommend buying a gift for someone who has helped you out along your way. It'll make them really happy.'

Right. Tomorrow I'll go out and look for something to send to Natsuko-san. And one other important thing . . . But I wonder where I'd find something she would like. In Tokyo, I suppose Ginza would make sense?

Kijima-san came with me as far as the main entrance to the Matsukiya department store facing Chuo Dori in Ginza. 'Umm, you're going to want to go in that direction. Are you sure you'll be OK? I could send a younger co-worker with you. I'd take you myself, but I have an appointment . . . Sorry.' She looked worried.

Fountain Pen

'I have the map you gave me, so I'll be OK. Plus, I have my phone. I'll manage!'

'I hope so. Oh, I'll call ahead to the shop. I'm sure he'll treat you well.' Kijima-san's kind gaze felt just like Natsuko-san's.

'OK, I'll be off, then.'

'No need to rush. Take your time! Call my mobile if you need anything. I'll find a way to help!'

She was like a mother sending her son on his first errand. It had only been a couple of hours since we met, but it felt like we had known each other far longer.

I set off, following the map she had drawn for me. It seemed like I could go straight down Chuo Dori for a while. When I turned around after walking for a bit, Kijima-san was still standing at the entrance to the department store. When I bobbed my head in thanks, she waved.

But wow, no one's ever given me a hand-drawn map before. I feel like these days people just tell you the website and that's it. The note with the map had the name of the shop, its address and Kijima-san's phone number.

After passing two sets of traffic lights, I turned down an alley near the third. In contrast to the glitzy main street, this alleyway was crammed with buildings and felt a bit maze-like. After walking for a little while, I turned at the second corner and found a cylindrical postbox.

It must have been getting repainted regularly; the brilliant vermilion really jumped out at you. I had only ever seen postboxes like this in movies or old TV shows; I could see why it made a good landmark. Behind it was the shop I was looking for.

'I guess this is the place . . .' I murmured to myself. I must

Letters from the Ginza Shihodo Stationery Shop

have been walking for ten minutes or so. Now that I had arrived, I could see it was just as the map had described, but for me, still new in Tokyo, it had been a bit of an adventure.

Kijima-san had told me it was a venerable old stationery shop, but though the three-storey building gave off an air of history, there was nothing run-down about it. It had style, but with restraint – there was something mysterious about the atmosphere. On the glass doors at the entrance, it said SHIHODO, in gold *kanji* characters.

A mild scent greeted me as I entered the shop. Maybe it was incense? Unlike a self-asserting cologne, this aroma wrapped me in a tenderness that soothed me amid all my struggles getting used to Tokyo.

A beat later, a man's voice sent an *Irasshaimase!* from the back of the shop. The greeting was gentle in the same way the incense was, and I felt like he was genuinely welcoming me from the bottom of his heart. It was the first time I'd ever heard such a pleasant 'irasshaimase'.

One of the things that bewildered me about Tokyo when I first arrived was 'irasshaimase'. In the countryside where I was born and raised, customers were greeted with a hello – *Konnichiwa*. Of course in the morning, they said good morning and at night they said good evening. I'm sure it had something to do with the nature of the region, that everyone knew each other, but if anyone said 'Irasshaimase', they were liable to get a, 'Oh-ho, you tryin' to sell me something?' With a smile, of course.

I got shrill calls of 'irasshaimase' at convenience stores, fast food joints and chain *izakaya*, certainly, but even at the bank and the ward office, and it wore me out.

Fountain Pen

But the 'irasshaimase' at this shop didn't have any of that unpleasantness. Why was that? I'm not sure. Maybe my relief at managing to find my way here had something to do with it.

Perhaps realising that I didn't seem very sure of myself, the owner of the voice appeared right away. A light blue shirt over grey slacks, a navy necktie, simple black leather shoes with laces. Hair that wasn't too long or too short, parted in a natural spot. He must have been in his mid-thirties or so?

'Umm, is this Shihodo?' I asked stupidly despite the fact that I had confirmed the name of the shop on the doors before coming in.

'Yes, this is Shihodo. Forgive me, but are you Nitta-sama?'

'Y-yes, that's me.'

'I've been expecting you. Were you able to find your way all right?'

'Yes, I managed. Thanks to this.'

The man looked at the scrap of paper I held out and gave a small nod. 'I'm glad. I received a call from Kijima-san a little while ago. She said she introduced Shihodo to an important customer named Nitta-sama and that I should make every effort to help him when he arrived,' he said before taking a business card out of his pocket and presenting it to me. 'Ken Takarada of Shihodo, at your service.'

'Oh, er, uh, nice to meet you . . .'

There's nothing that makes me more nervous as the shy guy I am than meeting someone for the first time. Whether Takarada-san realised how I felt inside or not, his gentle smile never wavered as he continued.

'To get right down to business, what can I do for you? Kijima-san just said, "I'm counting on you, Ken-chan!" and hung up on me.' That's always how she is, but . . . anyhow, she didn't tell me the nature of your errand.'

I suddenly returned to myself.

'Ohh, um, I'd like some stationery . . .'

Takarada-san nodded deeply as if to say, *Ah, just as I thought*, and a beat later replied, 'Understood.' Then with a relaxed air, he made a broad gesture towards the back of the store and added, 'Then, if you'll just follow me, most of the writing paper and envelopes are on the shelves over there.'

I wasn't sure why, but for some reason Takarada-san's relaxed but polite service was comfortable to me. Perhaps the brisk hospitality of simply attending to someone's business was something born of the wisdom of metropolitan people leading their busy lives, but that sort of service made me feel like I was being helped by a vending machine, and I didn't think I could get used to it.

The shelves he led me to were packed with paper and envelopes. A high-class paper that you could tell from a single glance was handmade *washi*, a fancy one made with pressed flowers, a light blue one with reddish-brown Western-style horizontal ruling – even just looking at them all made it seem like this would be fun.

Next to the papers were envelopes in the same design. There were long rectangular envelopes for vertical-use paper, and Western-sized envelopes for horizontal-use paper. At a cursory glance, it seemed like there were at least two hundred varieties.

'In addition to these, we have some that feature seasonal illustrations. And Western-style greeting cards are available near the postcards.'

'. . . There are so many kinds. I'm a little overwhelmed.'

Fountain Pen

'Thank you. There's limited space on the sales floor, so I'm not able to carry everything I'd like to. In terms of washi items and imported paper, I boast one of the widest selections in Tokyo. Of course, if there's anything I don't have, I can introduce you to larger stationery shops in Ginza, Nihonbashi or near Tokyo Station. Please tell me what you're looking for. I have a fairly good idea of what the other shops stock, and since I'm friendly with my colleagues in the industry, I can give them a call and have them set something aside for you.'

'Oh, no, I think it'll be hard enough for me to pick something here. I don't think I'll have the wherewithal to go look at other shops too.'

His little smile never wavering, Takarada-san picked up some paper. 'This one, *Tayori*, is pale white and features ten faintly drawn vertical lines, so it can be used for any purpose. Incidentally, it's a Shihodo original.'

'Oh, interesting.'

Takarada-san took down another type of paper from two shelves above. 'This one is called *Hagoromo*. This is another one exclusive to Shihodo. A washi artist said they wanted to create something for practical use and started this project, but the number available is quite limited . . . It's high-quality washi, and the lines are added during the paper-making process in a technique that makes them visible inside it. This can also be used for any purpose. Or another option would be . . . oh, sorry – I'm just showing you all the ones I'm personally fond of.'

Takarada-san's ever so polite manner was somewhat out of keeping for someone who seemed to be in his mid-thirties.

'They're both simple and elegant, really wonderful. Erm . . .'

Yes, I'm aware of how indecisive I am.

Letters from the Ginza Shihodo Stationery Shop

'Broadly speaking, there are two ways to select stationery. One is for the sender to choose something they like. Well, that's normal. The other is to choose something that would make the receiver happy. The two I recommended just now are the most standard of the standard, so you can't go wrong, but perhaps they're a little bland. So what if you considered the person you're sending to as you make your selection?'

'Ahh . . .'

I knew it was apt advice, but I had never written a real letter in my life. The most I'd done was a New Year's postcard.

'Since it was Kijima-san who referred you, you must be including a gift of some kind?' Takarada-san must have felt bad watching me flounder about, so he offered me a helping hand.

'Yes, I am. I just got my first pay cheque, so I was thinking I'd send a gift to my grandmother in the countryside. Coming to Ginza and looking at stuff was all well and good, but I had no idea what to get for her. As I was wandering around the food floor of a department store I had gone into at a total loss, a salesperson approached me.'

Takarada-san suddenly burst out laughing. 'Did she happen to say, "Whoa, hold on, hey, young man, are you all right?"'

'Yes! Exactly, exactly. She said, "Hey, young man, are you all right? You look so tired, and all that sweat. But look, it's the perfect season for cold-brewed *gyokuro*," and handed me a little paper cup of green tea. I was like "Huh?" but she had already pulled a chair out from the back – like "Here, take a seat and rest for a minute."'

Takarada-san nodded in amusement. 'When Kijima-san spots someone who looks tired or troubled, she can't leave them alone – that's just her nature.'

Fountain Pen

'Oh, hmm . . . And then, the tea she gave me was really delicious. It sounds like an exaggeration, but it was the first time in my life that I had had such sweet tea. I heaved a sigh without realising it, and she poured me a refill, saying, "What's wrong? Coming to Ginza of all places and sighing like that. Is something troubling you?"'

It was really strange. I'd only met Takarada-san a few minutes ago, but he was so easy to talk to. Come to think of it, Kijima-san was the same way. *Maybe I'm just blessed with encounters with kind people today.*

'Um, how old is Kijima-san?' I asked.

'Who can say? I refrain from asking women their ages, so I don't know. But she's been working at Matsukiya ever since I can remember, so she's probably getting on. I recall that she reached retirement age a few years ago. Since then, she's been helping out part-time doing staff training and looking after the important regular customers. Oh, and she's one of the few people on friendly enough terms with the president of the company to use *-kun*.'

'Wow, someone that illustrious talked to me?'

Takarada-san laughed with a small shake of his head. 'If you called her illustrious, I think she would get upset and say, "That makes me sound like a scary old lady!" Actually, she's only ever stern with herself and regarding work. With everyone else, no matter who, she's very kind. I aim to be like Kijima-san as a salesperson – no, as a human being.' He nodded emphatically before suddenly scratching the back of his head with a start. 'Sorry, I went off on a tangent.'

'Not at all! I wanted to tell someone how nice Kijima-san was to me, so I appreciate you listening to my story.'

Letters from the Ginza Shihodo Stationery Shop

Come to think of it, this might have been the first time I'd told someone the events of my day since coming to Tokyo three months prior. Before that, Natsuko-san had always listened, even when I just rambled pointlessly.

Once, at a meal during training, I was talking about how I got flustered when an automatic door wouldn't open for me, and one of my fellow trainees said, 'So what's the punchline?' When I trailed off in spite of myself, they laughed at me, and no one had my back, so my story ended there. Since then, I'd been scared to talk to anybody.

Takarada-san gave a little nod with a gentle smile hinting at his good nature and urged me to continue.

'After having the tea and calming down a little bit, I explained honestly how I had just been paid and wanted to send a gift to my grandmother in the countryside but wasn't sure what to get. She gave me a few different ideas, and I settled on tea.'

'It's first-harvest *shincha* season, and your grandmother will be reminded of how thoughtful you are every time she brews it, so I think that's a great choice,' he said, and then commented to himself, 'Shincha sounds good. I should go buy some later.'

'Yeah, I hadn't considered tea at all, so I'm grateful to Kijima-san for suggesting it. Anyhow, it was great to have decided on a gift, but then she says, "You should write her a letter to go with it." I'm connected to my grandmother online, so I figured sending a message like, "I sent you some tea from a department store!" would be enough, but Kijima-san told me, "Simple is fine, but do write something – as a favour to me!"'

Takarada-san hmmed with a deep nod. 'And then she referred you to Shihodo, huh?'

'Yes. She said, "We have a stationery section here, but the

Fountain Pen

selection isn't very good. I'll refer you to a specialist shop called Shihodo, so go talk to the manager." She drew me the map, too.' Takarada-san smiled and replied, 'I'll have to thank her.'

'So yes, I'm looking for paper and envelopes.'

'Understood. Then how about this one? Forgive me for recommending all Shihodo originals, but the lines on this one are nicely spaced, giving you plenty of room to write, so it's perfect for your purpose today.'

The paper he handed me was light green with eight lines. The boxes on the envelopes where the postcode was meant to go were the same colour as the lines, and the space to stick the stamp featured an illustration of fresh green leaves growing from a branch.

'This colour is called *wakabairo* after new leaves. This product is called *Tsukizuki*, and the design comes in twelve different colours. The lines grow fainter as you reach the bottom.' He peeled up the cover to show me. The lines seemed to be drawn by someone with a very fine brush and grew fainter and thinner on their way down the page. By the bottom, there was hardly a line there at all.

'This series came about when a painter in the *Nihonga* style requested letter paper with room to paint a little something. Incidentally, the lines and the illustrations by the stamp were provided by that same customer, who said, "I'm the one making the request, so I'll help out!" The twelve colours were also selected by that customer. There are 465 traditional Japanese colours, so I think it must have been difficult to choose only twelve. There's the matter of how they look against the base colour to consider, too. That said, this product was launched by a much earlier generation's manager, so I don't know who the painter was.'

Letters from the Ginza Shihodo Stationery Shop

He showed me the other Tsukizuki colours: brownish-red *azukiiro* and magenta *koshi*, pink *nadeshikoiro*, blue *aofujiiro* and persimmon *kakiiro*, crimson *kurenai*, greyish-brown *susutakeiro*, reddish-brown *ebicha*, peachy *akebonoiro* plus silvery-grey *ginnezu* and, finally, golden *konjiki*.

'They're all the same price except for konjiki because it uses gold leaf. I apologise, but the price of gold keeps going up ... And there aren't as many artisans these days, either. We may have to give up on foil stamping someday.'

They were all nice colours and easy on the eye, too. I wondered why the gentle pigments felt so soothing to my eyes.

The envelopes came in packs of five wrapped in a paper band. The illustrations in the stamp corner were all adorable: three azuki beans for azukiiro, the light of the rising sun for akebonoiro, Mount Fuji for konjiki.

Takarada-san seemed to notice I was eyeing the illustrations.

'Some of our customers say it's a shame to cover up the illustration, so they stick the stamp to the side. It's happened so often that the postal worker who comes here for deliveries has grumbled more than once that I need to "Please make sure they affix the stamp in the correct position."'

'I get how they feel, though. Oh, but since I'm putting it in with the tea, I won't need a stamp. All right, I'll take the wakabairo paper and envelopes please.'

Takarada-san said, 'Very well. Thank you,' before taking the products from my hands and saying, 'Right this way.'

On the way to the counter, he asked, 'Oh, I don't mean to be intrusive, but do you have something to write with?'

I replied with a nod. 'I wanted to ask you about that. I'm hoping for some ink to go with this.'

Fountain Pen

I dug my hand into my backpack and pulled out a long, slim gift box. It had a black slip featuring a white logo, and inside was a fountain pen.

Takarada-san went behind the counter and set the stationery I had chosen to the side. 'One moment, please,' he said, and took a pair of white gloves out of a drawer. Then he took out a rectangular tray-like piece of wood, set it on the counter, and put the gloves on. There was felt pasted inside the tray, so it was like a work space for handling precious objects.

'If I may,' he said concisely before using both hands to accept the box I held out. Then he set it gently on the work space, pulled a chair up from behind him and sat down.

'I beg your pardon, but if I work standing up and my hand slips, I'm afraid I might damage it. So while I don't mean to seat myself in front of a customer, please allow me to sit down. You may use that chair there if you wish.' He indicated a chair next to the counter with his gaze. I moved it over to sit across from him.

'A Montblanc, I see. But not a recent model.'

'That's right.'

He gingerly removed the gift box from its sleeve. The top of the box had the so-called 'white star' brand emblem on it. When he opened the lid, there was the instruction booklet and the warranty, and beneath that lay the fountain pen. The pen was on a fabric cushion, and its cap's clip and ring gleamed golden.

'So, I don't know much about fountain pens, but this is a high-quality one, right? Like, famous authors used them . . . ?' I asked.

Takarada-san nodded. 'Yes, broadly speaking, that is correct. This is a Montblanc Meisterstück Classique. Its relatively slim barrel means it can be naturally slipped into a suit jacket's inner pocket, and since our hands tend to be smaller than Westerners', it's the perfect fountain pen for Japanese people.'

'Ohh.'

It felt a little strange having a lesson on my own property.

'Authors, as you mentioned earlier, and others who make writing their occupation, seem to prefer a slightly thicker barrel. For example, this is also a Meisterstück, but the Le Grand 146.'

He took a fountain pen out of the showcase at the side of the counter. The silhouette closely resembled mine, but was slightly larger overall. The thickness of the barrel, especially, was completely different.

'The diameter of your Classique's barrel is 12 millimetres, whereas this one's is 13.3. They say this thickness is suitable for longer periods of writing.'

I took the Le Grand 146 when he held it out.

'It certainly is thick. I feel like mine is thick compared to the ballpoint pens and mechanical pencils I usually use, but this one is beyond even that.'

'Indeed,' said Takarada-san as he took out another pen. 'The thickest is 15.2 millimetres. It's called the Meisterstück 149 and is similarly popular among writers while also used to sign international treaties, major contracts between corporations, and other such documents. I feel it's a bit majestic for daily use, but it's perfect for those times you want that extra solemnity.'

The 149 he held out felt almost like a permanent marker in terms of thickness.

While I was looking at the other pens, Takarada-san took the cap off the one I'd entrusted him with and then twisted the body to split it in two right around the middle and remove the long, narrow part inside.

Fountain Pen

'The tip and converter are both clean. Or rather, you've never used this, have you?'

'You're right, I've actually never used it before.'

Nodding at my reply, he held the ink cartridge that came in the gift box up to the light and shook it.

'I'm not sure if you'll be able to use this ink. Ummm, the date of the warranty is . . . let's see. Ahh, twelve whole years ago.'

'Yes, my grandmother gave it to me when I was ten.'

Takarada-san looked a little surprised. 'Ten would have put you in . . . fourth grade? It's terribly impolite of me to say so, but I think this is a rather fine instrument to give to an elementary schooler.'

'Right? So while I was happy to receive it, I couldn't very well take it to school. I put it away deep in a drawer and had actually forgotten about it altogether until recently.'

'I see. Well, it's brand new and doesn't seem to have a scratch, so if you fill it with new ink you should be able to use it without any issues. By the way, if you're going to use this converter, I recommend bottled ink. If you think you'll use it out and about often, cartridges are handy. Which do you prefer?'

'Which makes it easier to take care of?'

'Once you get used to the process, neither way is very difficult, but if I had to choose, I'd say cartridges are more convenient.'

'Then I'll take cartridges, please.'

Takarada-san said, 'Just a moment,' and came out from behind the counter to go to what must have been the writing instrument shelves and brought back several small boxes. 'Recently, Montblanc has been releasing all sorts of playful colours, but for a letter, I think a standard colour would be best. From the right, I have Mystery Black, Midnight Blue and Royal Blue.

Letters from the Ginza Shihodo Stationery Shop

The farther to the left, the brighter and bluer. I also have green and purple, but the use cases for those are more limited.'

'Which is the safest?'

'There's no one answer, but the colour that came packaged with your pen is Midnight Blue. They used to call it Blue/Black.'

Sure enough, the cartridge he said I shouldn't use said 'Blue/Black' on it, in English.

'Then I'd like to have that one.'

'Very good.'

My total came to a little over 2,000 yen. At the department store, the tea, with shipping included, had been a few thousand yen. I had come to Ginza expecting to spend quite a bit on my grandmother's present and ink for my fountain pen, but, surprisingly, I hadn't done too badly. I was sure it was because I'd been blessed to cross paths with such nice people.

After I paid, I was waiting for my change when Takarada-san asked, 'Um, you're going to put the letter in with the tea, right? So you'll write somewhere before going back to Matsukiya?'

'Yes, that's my plan. Kijima-san said if I got it to her by 6 p.m. she would pack it with the tea and send my package with today's shipment.'

'Then, this is just an idea, but . . . why don't you write here up on the first floor? I rent the space out for workshops in paper craft, calligraphy, seal-carving and so on, but there aren't any events today. And I have the perfect desk and chair for a comfortable writing session.'

The sudden invitation caught me off guard, but it made me happy, too.

'R-Really? I was about to ask if you knew a comfortable cafe nearby.'

Fountain Pen

Takarada-san nodded. 'Yes, by all means, use the first floor. Oh, but of course, there are also good cafes in the neighbourhood that I can recommend. The one I go to often is called *Hohozue*. The coffee and tea are delicious, of course, but so is the food. So if you're feeling thirsty and want to put something in your stomach, I can introduce you. But it's not a good place to write an important letter to your grandmother. After all, the tables and chairs there are made for relaxing with a drink.'

'. . . Ah, I feel sort of bad.'

I hung my head. It would have been better to say thank you . . .

Takarada-san waved me off in a hurry. 'None of that! It can't be good luck for me to make a customer feel that way!' he said. 'But first, here are your purchases and your receipt.'

He set my change on a little leather tray and slid it towards me. New 1,000-yen bills, new coins. I couldn't help but 'wow' in admiration. 'I didn't know coins could be this pretty.'

'I feel the same way. The 500-yen coin especially is so shiny I almost want to wear it around my neck as a pendant. Incidentally, the 500-yen coin is made of this mix of 60 per cent copper and 40 per cent zinc called brass.'

'Do you always return change in new money?'

Takarada-san answered yes as if it were the most natural thing in the world. 'It takes extra effort, and there's a fee to pay, but I do it because I enjoy seeing customers' surprised smiles. Though these days many people opt for cashless payment, so the money makes fewer appearances,' he said with a glum expression.

'Somehow, I feel like it would be a shame to put these in

Letters from the Ginza Shihodo Stationery Shop

my wallet with my other change. And it would be a waste to fold the bills.'

I had a folding wallet with a coin pocket in the centre. It had been fine for cramming into my back pocket as a student, but nowadays it was annoying because I had to reach my hand in deep to fish it out of the inner pocket of my suit jacket.

'Well, it's only a stopgap, but let's do this,' said Takarada-san as he poured the coins into a plastic zip lock bag and put the bills into a postcard-sized paper bag.

'Ahh, sorry . . .'

All I've been saying is sorry, sorry, sorry. Maybe it's just what I say. As I said it, I took the foreign mystery I was reading out of my backpack and slipped the new bills between its pages. I put the coins in the bottom of my backpack.

'*She Rides Shotgun?* That's a good one.'

I didn't have it in a cover, but I was still surprised Takarada-san said the title at a single glance.

'You've read it?'

'Yes. From the placement of your bookmark, you still have a lot to look forward to.'

I felt kind of happy. Up to now, I hadn't really encountered anyone with the same interests as me. There are groups online, on social media and whatnot, where people into the hardboiled genre and foreign mysteries gather, but I've only ever lurked; I never post, myself. My friends give me weird looks, but I can't help but feel a little anxious about revealing my personal thoughts to people I've never met.

I seem to be a rare sort these days, though. Some people even think, 'I'd hate it if I said what I really thought to my friends and it weirded them out, so it's actually easier to be honest with

Fountain Pen

people I don't know.' But every time I hear people say that, I think, *Then what am I to you? Are you telling me what you really think or just being polite?*

'OK, allow me to escort you to the first floor.'

I'd been spacing out, so I jumped when Takarada-san spoke.

As he left the register, he put out a desk bell and a little plaque that read: I'M CURRENTLY ON ANOTHER FLOOR. PLEASE RING FOR SERVICE. Then he said, 'Right this way,' and led me to the rear of the shop.

Past the stationery area he originally showed me, we came to a staircase. A sign standing in front of it read: TODAY'S WORKSHOPS HAVE ENDED.

Passing by the signpost, we began to climb the stairs; partway up there was a spacious landing of maybe three or four square metres with a chair and a little coffee table. The chair seemed like the perfect place from which to gaze absentmindedly at the sales floor below.

'Some longtime customers enjoy sitting here for a cup of tea.'

'It does seem comfortable.'

Takarada-san's lips raised slightly in a smile, and he said, 'Just a little farther now.' As if we were mountain-climbing. I found it so amusing I laughed.

The windows on the first floor were larger than those on the ground floor, so it was bright even with no lights on thanks to the brilliant spring sunlight. There should have been just the same amount of floor space as downstairs, but the first floor seemed larger, in part due to the absence of product displays and so on. Towards the windows on the right was a raised four-and-a-half-tatami-mat area. In the centre of the room were six worktables on casters arranged in a rectangle with two chairs at each table.

Letters from the Ginza Shihodo Stationery Shop

The entire left-hand wall from floor to ceiling was drawers of all different sizes.

'That's the desk.'

In the direction Takarada-san pointed, a desk with a dignified atmosphere and a chair made from the same type of wood were waiting for me. There was nothing on the desktop, and it was bathed in the light streaming in from between the blinds.

I followed Takarada-san towards the desk. It seemed very well used, with lots of little scratches here and there. On the right side, perhaps someone had tipped over an ink bottle – there was a black stain. Takarada-san pulled out the chair and said, 'Have a seat.'

I sat down as instructed. The seat was upholstered in leather and stuffed firm. But it was a comfortable firmness. I tried putting my elbows on the desk. Though its surface gleamed, I could sense the subtle grain in the wood where my arms made contact.

Takarada-san opened the middle left-hand drawer. There were ten or so books inside. 'You'll find classic books on letter writing etiquette, dictionaries and so on in here.'

That was a bit of a relief. I didn't feel like I would be able to write something without a reference.

'Thank you. I'll be quick,' I replied, taking the fountain pen box and the stationery and ink cartridges I had just bought from my backpack on the floor.

'No, you mustn't rush. You told Kijima-san you'd be back by six, right? You still have hours. Please take your time and write carefully. After all, handwritten characters have expressions. They have laughing faces, crying faces, angry faces, happy faces, kind faces ... Your mood at the time will be expressed directly.'

Fountain Pen

'... Expressions?'

I'd never considered that. But it's true that everyone's handwriting is unique to them. I'd been communicating so much via LINE chat and email that I didn't have very many chances to see handwritten characters anymore.

Takarada-san said, 'Just a moment,' and went to get something from a drawer nearby. It seemed that the drawers along the wall were for storing inventory.

'Please use this as a thank-you for coming to the shop ... and a present to commemorate meeting a fellow lover of translated hardboiled fiction. A notebook produced by Shihodo.'

'Y-You're giving it to me? Are you sure?'

'Of course,' he said with a little nod.

The notebook he set on the desk had NOTE printed in small letters on its light grey cover and a couple of unobtrusive lines for writing a title and name. The spine was black with a cream-coloured label. It seemed as thick as two regular notebooks.

'I'm not sure I'm worthy.'

I opened the new notebook. The paper was just the right thickness and pleasant to the touch.

'First, I recommend writing down whatever words and characters come to mind. You can think of how to arrange the text later. If you feel like you made a mistake or something didn't capture your thoughts, cross it out with a single line. It's important to make sure you can read it again, since you might think, "Oh, maybe I'll use this after all." No one but you will look at your notebook, so there's no need to write neatly. Just put down every word that comes to mind. That's key.'

'Put down every word ...'

Letters from the Ginza Shihodo Stationery Shop

'I think the pen will grow accustomed to your hand as you write. Oh, try installing a cartridge. Hopefully the ink will flow smoothly...'

I took the fountain pen and a cartridge out of their respective boxes as instructed.

'Uh, so now what do I do?'

'First, remove the cap. Montblanc caps are threaded, so twist the top to unscrew it. Then unscrew the section from the barrel. Yes, that's right. Then put the thinner end of the cartridge into the section – you'll feel some resistance, but push it in all the way.'

I tried doing what he said. *Aha.* It did sort of feel like it was getting stuck, but when I added some force, it slid in.

'Incidentally, you can store a spare cartridge inside the barrel.'

I slipped a spare into the barrel as he suggested and then screwed the section back in. Then I put the cap on top of the other end and tried holding the pen.

'Use this to draw some circles to get the ink flowing.'

He took a memo pad out of a desk drawer and ripped a sheet off for me. I ran the pen over it as instructed. The gold-trimmed nib glided effortlessly across the paper. Soon a trail of ink began to follow it in circles.

'Wow.' I was surprised. It felt different from writing with a pencil or ballpoint pen, and refreshing. I enjoyed it so much I doodled some spirals, wrote some *hiragana* characters, plus some random words like 'Tokyo'.

'What do you think?'

'It's my first time using a fountain pen, so I'm not sure what to say, but it's refreshing, somehow. It doesn't take much pressure

Fountain Pen

to change the force, and I don't really know how to explain it, but I feel like it makes my handwriting better.'

Takarada-san nodded a number of times, looking as happy as if he himself were being complimented. 'Unlike pencils and ballpoint pens, which need to be pressed against the paper to write, fountain pens employ capillary action, so as long as the nib is touching the paper, it will write. A larger contact surface area will give you thicker, bolder strokes, while a smaller contact surface area will yield slimmer, weaker lines – the writer can make these subtle adjustments at will. In other words, a fountain pen is similar to a brush dipped in ink.'

'. . . I see. I had no idea.'

'Sorry to ramble on with unnecessary details. Well, I think your ink is flowing smoothly now. Please use the notebook,' he urged. Then he pointed at the door next to the staircase. 'The bathroom is over there. Feel free to use it. I'll be on the ground floor, but I'll bring up some tea in a bit. Oh, but Shihodo isn't a cafe so I can't vouch for the flavour. It's on the house, though, so it won't cost you anything.' Ending with a 'Take your time', he descended the stairs.

Once Takarada-san receded from view, I straightened up and confronted the notebook. The white paper was ruled with light grey lines. The width seemed to be about a centimetre. When I looked at the back cover, it said *A4, UL ruled*. I'd heard of A and B ruling before, but UL was a first. Still, maybe these lines were the perfect size to scribble down whatever came to mind.

I picked up the Montblanc again and wrote the date in the upper-left-hand corner. *Yeah, writing with this is so comfy.*

Then I added, *Rough Draft: Letter to Grandmother.* I kind

Letters from the Ginza Shihodo Stationery Shop

of felt like I was trying to act too cool, so as Takarada-san had explained to me, I drew a single line through '*Grandmother*' and wrote '*Natsuko-san*' above it.

I was born when my grandmother was fifty years old. She must not have wanted to be called 'Grandma' yet. Or maybe she didn't want to make me overly conscious of my situation by having me call her 'Grandma'. I'm not sure what her reasoning was, but she always insisted that I call her 'Natsuko-san'. Despite that, she would say, 'I don't much care for the name Natsuko.' Apparently, she was the second of four sisters, and her mother had named the first Haruko, for spring, so she received the name Natsuko, for summer.

'My sister was born in March, so they named her Haruko, but then I automatically become Natsuko just because I'm second? I've wondered any number of times what that was about. I was born in December, you know! Akiko was born in April, not autumn, and Fuyuko was born in July, not winter. They both made the same complaints. But oh well. People just name their kids whatever they want.'

Natsuko-san had talked to me about this issue numerous times.

'By the way, I was the one who named you Rin – because I wanted you to conduct yourself with "dignity" always.'

I'm pretty sure she told me about that during the summer I was a fourth-grader.

We were going to have a Coming Halfway of Age Ceremony at the culture festival in autumn, so part of our summer homework was to ask our guardian about the origin of our name. Thinking back on it now, I wish they had been a little more considerate of the fact that every household has different

Fountain Pen

circumstances. By that time, I was vaguely aware that my mother, unable to take care of me on her own, had left me with Natsuko-san. As a ten-year-old, I had mixed feelings – both wanting and not wanting to know at the same time – but I really hated being forced to look into my family as homework.

Natsuko-san didn't seem upset as she explained, though: how her one daughter had returned home with a big belly. How the father had a wife and kids and broke his promise to get a divorce and be with her. How the labour had been quite difficult. How when I was about a year old, my mother got a job in the next town over. How she married a different man before long, but that he didn't want me in the picture. How, until I was around three years old, she had come to see me once a month, but that we'd become estranged when her husband got transferred and they moved away.

And then . . .

'Do you want to see her?' she asked me.

'Meh.'

That vague reaction was all I could muster.

'But wow, you're already ten, huh? Time flies. Not so long ago you were *this* tiny! No wonder I'm turning sixty,' she said with a wince. 'A Coming Halfway of Age Ceremony, though, eh? Your school comes up with some pretty fancy ideas.'

'You think so? But it's not anything like actually coming of age. It's not like you're allowed to do anything you weren't allowed to do before . . . Nothing good happens at all, it's just a bunch of obnoxious homework.'

'Hmm. I'm happy, though, because it gives me another excuse to celebrate you. After all, when you turn twenty, I'll be a seventy-year-old grandma! I don't even know if I'll be alive!'

Letters from the Ginza Shihodo Stationery Shop

'Don't go jinxing yourself! I'm sure you'll be fit as a fiddle.'

'I hope so . . .' She thought to herself for a little while and then said, 'OK!' with an emphatic nod. 'Let's do something together to celebrate!'

'Huh? Celebrate what?'

'Your coming halfway of age and my sixtieth birthday, obviously! Oh, that's what we'll do! Tomorrow I'll close up the shop and we'll go on an outing. We'll take the train somewhere.'

This was an utterly unexpected thing for her to say.

Incidentally, up to that point, I have no memories of going out anywhere with Natsuko-san. She ran a little pharmacy on the ground floor of her house and almost never closed it.

'It's just a tiny shop, but it's the only pharmacy in town. Sickness and injury don't care if it's your day off.'

That was her way of doing things, so apart from about two days each for Obon and New Year's, she kept the shop open, including weekends and holidays. That said, even if it was her day off or the middle of the night, if someone knocked on the door, she helped them, so in practice, she was open year-round.

When I would get home from school, I used to sit on the bench out front and wait absentmindedly for a customer to show up. Watching the people, cars and delivery trucks passing by, I was never bored.

So I wasn't really sure what Natsuko-san meant when she said we would go on an 'outing'. That's how rare it was for us to go anywhere.

The next day after breakfast, she handed me a brand-new polo shirt and said, 'Change into this.' I had no idea when she had bought it, but I remember being delighted because it had the logo of my favourite football team embroidered on the chest.

Fountain Pen

'You've never really ridden a bus or train before, so take this just in case, Rin.' I remember that was the first time I took motion-sickness pills.

The bus to the station took half an hour; then we rode a train for an hour. We arrived at a city with a department store a little before noon.

'First, let's fortify our bellies.' With that, Natsuko-san headed for the big restaurant on the top floor. I think the building had about ten floors; the restaurant had a good view, so we spent the time until the food arrived looking out of the windows. Natsuko-san pointed out different things, like, 'That's the Prefectural Government Office,' and 'We can see way into the distance because the air is clear today.'

At the sound of a voice saying, 'Apologies for the wait,' I turned my eyes back to the table to find a *yoshoku* plate lunch featuring a Hamburg steak and a breaded shrimp.

'I could make Hamburg steaks and breaded shrimp at home if I wanted to, but those things never taste as good as what you can get at a restaurant. Yoshoku is by far the best choice when eating out,' said Natsuko-san. She slathered her shrimp in tartare sauce and chowed down in high spirits, looking like she really enjoyed it.

Then we took the escalator and stopped to walk around each floor on our way down.

I don't really remember all the details, but it was a countryside *hyakkaten*, a department store living up to the kanji in the word – 'plethora of products' – by selling every last thing you could possibly want: bedding, furniture, travel goods, cooking utensils and dishes, household appliances, toys, plus clothing and cosmetics . . . Even just walking around oohing and ahhing or making jokes like, 'Does anyone really buy these things?' was fun in itself.

Partway down was the stationery department. The showcases were full of expensive-looking pens both fountain and ballpoint, and the whole place gave off an aura that made me feel like children weren't allowed to just wander in. The next section over was highlighters, so regardless of whether Natsuko-san was interested or not, there definitely wasn't anything there I wanted to look at.

She walked to the back of the stationery shop and stared at the showcase before murmuring, 'Right, a Montblanc it is.'

'Hm? What's a Mont Blanc? Like the cake?'

'It's nothing. Let's go.'

Then we swiftly left that department.

Later, when we found the toys, Natsuko-san said, 'I want to go take a look at the makeup, so can you wait here? I'll be back in fifteen minutes,' and off she went without me.

My memories of our outing abruptly cut off at this scene. I'm sure she came back in less than half an hour, and then we must have immediately headed home, but I don't really remember.

That was the only time I ever went on an outing with Natsuko-san.

As part of the culture festival in October, we had the Coming Halfway of Age Ceremony. I don't remember exactly what sort of ceremony it was, but the one thing I do remember is that Natsuko-san closed the pharmacy and came to see it.

For dinner that night, she made celebratory red bean rice. And the two of us clinked glasses of soda – also a rare treat – to say cheers.

Fountain Pen

'When you turn twenty, we'll say cheers with real alcohol!'

'I'm not sure you need to announce that while I'm still ten, but OK!'

As I was laughing, Natsuko-san handed me a little package and said, 'This is for you.' The wrapping paper was from the department store we had visited together over the summer holiday.

'What is it?'

'Open it.'

I undid the ribbon and carefully removed the wrapping paper to find an expensive-looking box wrapped in a pretty sleeve. There was a white star-shaped logo on the box. When I gently lifted the lid, a fountain pen was sitting on shiny fabric.

'... This is what you were looking at in the department store, isn't it?'

'Yes, a Montblanc fountain pen.'

When I picked it up, I saw that the barrel was engraved with little golden letters: *R.N.*

'I had them put your initials there. Or, I guess, they offer that service. The shop employee said they could also do my initial and your initial, N to R, but I was embarrassed so I didn't pick that option,' said Natsuko-san with a smile.

'Wow, but aren't these expensive?'

'Well, they're not cheap. But if you take good care of it, they say it'll last a lifetime. And wasn't it Shotaro Ikenami who said, " A pen is the modern man's *katana*"? He's a famous historical fiction author. So I thought I should give you a good one, Rin.'

'Oh, thank you. I'll take good care of it. But I guess I can't use it at school . . .'

'Well, how about you use it to write a love letter when

you find someone you like? You can keep it tucked away until then. It's not as if it will go bad or something. OK, let's eat our red bean rice!'

When I looked up, I saw that, though she was smiling, Natsuko-san's eyes were filled with tears threatening to overflow. Normally I would ask *Why are you crying?* to tease her, but this time, for some reason, I decided I had better not say anything.

I looked down at the notebook and saw the words: *department store, Hamburg steak and breaded shrimp, Coming Halfway of Age Ceremony, red bean rice, Montblanc fountain pen*. I drew a big circle around them.

Suddenly I heard animated voices outside, so I looked out of the window onto the street below. Some boys in uniforms – maybe middle-schoolers? – were kicking a football as they walked past. They seemed out of place in Ginza, but when I searched on my phone, I found there was a middle school near Shinbashi Station, so I figured they must have been on their way home from there.

As a middle-schooler, I didn't have any major rebellious period, remaining comparatively obedient as I grew up. Maybe I felt indebted to Natsuko-san on some level for taking the pain to raise me.

Just once, on our way home from a meeting with my teacher during my second year of middle school, we got into a fight and I blurted out, 'You're not even my mum!' Even now I have a clear memory of how sad she looked in that moment. It's not exactly 'a hedge between keeps friendships green', but it's precisely because we're so close that some words should never be

Fountain Pen

spoken. Yet she didn't snap back at me, but just let it go out the other ear in silence. Her mature handling of the situation made me feel even worse.

For high school and university, I was blessed with schools I could commute to from home. That said, it was a two-hour trip each way; during high school I did all that plus club activities, and in university, it was hard to balance with my research and my part-time job. My tuition was covered by scholarships, so that worked out, but I didn't feel like I could ask Natsuko-san for money to cover lodgings. And Natsuko-san never told me to get out. She would wake early to eat breakfast with me and make me a packed lunch.

'Don't worry! I'll make sure none of your friends tease you for having an old person *bento*!'

She made that pronouncement without a peep from me and then used books, magazines and websites to prep me colourful lunches every day.

'I get a nice lunch, too, so it's two birds with one stone,' she said with a smile, but I'm sure it was hard work.

Natsuko-san's fried chicken, mini Hamburg steaks and mille-feuille katsu are all exquisite and my friends often begged me for a bite. Her side dishes – potato salad, carrot and scrambled egg, burdock root, sweet and spicy lotus root stir-fry – were all tasty, too, so I always looked forward to lunch.

Aside from those items she would also always include two big rice balls: one filled with pickled plum, the other with salted seaweed. The plum one was wrapped in toasted seaweed, while the seaweed one was coated in bits of dried kelp. Each one was easily as big as two regular rice balls, so they carried me through till dinner time, even on days I had club activities.

Letters from the Ginza Shihodo Stationery Shop

Since moving out, I've been buying convenience store rice balls. The first time I picked one up, I was shocked at how light it was. But it makes sense. There are a lot of people in the city who worry about overeating. Me, I can eat five of the things and it's still not enough, but they're expensive, so I restrict myself to three. Maybe that's why I have dreams about chomping into one of the rice balls Natsuko-san used to make for me.

When I moved to Tokyo for work, I was annoyed by how incapable I was. About a month before I left home, I asked Natsuko-san to give me a few lessons in housework, so I can manage cleaning and laundry all right, but I'm a hopeless cook.

I did learn how to use a rice cooker, at least, so for the rest I make do with instant miso soup and prepared foods from the store. There are a variety of supermarkets and convenience stores near my apartment, and I've tried the food at all of them, but I can't get used to any of the flavours. The dishes fill my stomach, but I never feel relaxed after eating. Since coming to Tokyo, I don't think I've eaten a single thing that soothed my soul.

That was part of the reason that for lunch on this day, I splurged on a venerable yoshoku restaurant's famous chicken rice with breaded shrimp. It came with consommé soup and a mini salad, but the price was a bit of a shock; I decided to think of it as a reward for myself. I had no complaints about the flavour, and for some reason it reminded me of the Hamburg steak and shrimp I'd eaten with Natsuko-san that time we went to the department store.

And I wished I could have eaten it with her. *I wonder what Natsuko-san had for lunch today...*

*

Fountain Pen

When I lifted my gaze from the notebook, I saw a tea bowl at the edge of the desk alongside a perfectly white moist towel rolled up on a narrow bamboo tray plus a sweet red bean paste sandwich made with little pancakes. Next to it was a handwritten note that said, *Please enjoy when you're ready for a break.*

When did Takarada-san bring that up? I hadn't even noticed. My friends during school and my current co-workers laugh at me: 'When you focus, you lose sight of your surroundings, Rin.' In a way, that meant I wasn't taking care of myself, so it felt like a shameless way to act in the position of being treated so kindly at a stationery shop I was visiting for the first time, borrowing a desk and all. Even I had to be embarrassed.

On the paper in front of me I had added words like: *meeting with teacher, first fight, fried chicken, carrot and scrambled eggs.* In some places the characters were bleeding or blurred. I had noticed I was crying, but I was scared to press my hands to my eyes because I feared that if I did the tears might not stop.

The towel was pleasantly chilled. Steam rose from the tea bowl. It couldn't have been long since Takarada-san had prepared it. I spread out the towel and pressed it over my face. The coolness felt nice against my puffy, post-cry eyelids.

The day before I left for Tokyo, Natsuko-san said, 'I won't be able to cook for you for a while, so . . .' and made all my favourite foods plus our first red bean rice since my Coming Halfway of Age Ceremony.

Natsuko-san and I couldn't get our schedules to line up, so her 70th birthday and my Coming of Age Ceremony had passed without celebration. Or more accurately, I prioritised research and my part-time job and didn't make time for her . . .

Letters from the Ginza Shihodo Stationery Shop

Natsuko-san watched in delight as I plucked bites from all the different dishes arranged on the table.

'You should eat, too, Natsuko-san.'

'. . . Yes. I will,' she nodded as she sipped the rest of the beer we'd toasted with.

'C'mon, what's wrong? Are you not feeling well?'

'Huh? Yeah. Mm, maybe I'm tired from cooking so much at once,' she laughed weakly. 'Rin, I wanted to say . . .'

'Yes?'

'Mm, never mind . . . You must be looking forward to Tokyo,' she said. 'Tokyo . . . I'd like to go for a visit someday.'

'You should!'

She shook her head. 'Even I've been to Tokyo before! Of course, that was decades ago, but . . .'

'Oh.'

The conversation lulled. The only sound at the table was the tick-tocking of the old pendulum clock on the wall.

How many minutes passed? Eventually I set down my chopsticks and said, 'Um, Natsuko-san . . .'

'Hm?'

'Um, well . . . There's something that's always been on my mind. You remember that time in middle school I was mean to you? I'm sorry. I've always wanted to apologise to you for saying, "You're not even my mum."'

Natsuko-san looked surprised for a moment but then smiled. 'You were worried about that?'

'. . . I mean, it was such an awful thing to say.'

She shook her head lightly and looked at me. 'Honestly, I was a bit sad. But when I thought about it, your mother said far worse things far more often, so I decided it wasn't really a big deal.

Fountain Pen

On the contrary, I was actually sort of happy.'

'Happy?'

'Yes. You always held yourself back around me, so I was glad to see you acting self-centred for once.'

'I have no idea what you're talking about . . .'

Those were the only words I could muster. Really, there was something else I wanted to say, but I missed my chance.

'Rin, I owe you an apology, too.' She put down the cup she was holding and sat up straight. 'Back around the time of your Coming Halfway of Age Ceremony, your mother showed up and said she wanted to take you back.'

'. . . Really?'

'Yes. Her husband was being transferred overseas and she was trying to decide whether to go with him or not. She said she had the option to send him on his own and take you back and live together, just the two of you in Japan. She said if she went overseas, she wouldn't be back within ten years, so she would lose her chance to live with you.'

I had never heard about this.

'"You're so selfish!" I thought. I was irritated. But since she was your actual mother, I wasn't sure what to do. She said she wanted to talk to you, but I decided that an emotional ten-year-old wouldn't be capable of making a level-headed decision. So we were talking past each other. Then I suggested we make a bet.'

'A bet?'

She nodded as she continued. 'Do you remember when we went to the department store that summer?'

'. . . Yeah.' It was hard to say anything, so I kept it brief.

'I left you in the toy department for a little while on your own, right?'

Letters from the Ginza Shihodo Stationery Shop

'Yeah, you said you were going to look at the makeup or something. Like, "I'll be right back so wait here."'

'Well, your mother was standing right there.'

I had no words.

'Our deal was that if she said hello and you said, "Mum?" I would give you back to her . . .' Her eyes overflowed with tears. 'That year I had just turned sixty, and one of my old schoolmates passed away, so I was feeling anxious about whether I would live until you were ready to venture out on your own, but I also really wanted to keep you with me. I really wasn't sure what to do when she approached me. That's why I decided to propose the bet, but I was terrified to find out how it turned out . . . I practically fled up the escalator. And that was when I ordered the fountain pen.'

Natsuko-san didn't seem to realise it, but she kept referring to my mother as if she were a stranger.

Pressing a tissue to her eyes, she continued. 'When I went back to the toy department after twenty minutes, I was relieved to find you completely absorbed in the plastic models. I remember I nearly crumpled on the spot. Afterwards, she gave me a call and said she didn't even manage to speak to you, that it had been a mistake to stay away for seven whole years.'

'I see . . .'

'I'm sorry, Rin. I should have made space for you two to talk. If I had, you might have led a different life. I'm so sorry.'

'No . . . it's OK.' That was all I could muster. 'Thanks for cooking,' I said, and left Natsuko-san to go to my room.

I'd already shipped most of my belongings, so my room felt empty.

Recalling the fountain pen, I dug around in my desk drawer.

Fountain Pen

And there it was, the Montblanc I'd put away all those years ago. I tucked it into my backpack and snuggled into my futon early.

I fell asleep to the sound of Natsuko-san doing the dishes downstairs.

When I finished writing the final draft of the letter, it was four-thirty.

I had started by saying, *Dear Natsuko-san, How are you doing? I'm doing well.* Then I wrote about the events of the day: about how I received my first pay cheque that Friday. How a more senior co-worker recommended buying a gift for someone who had helped us out along our way and how I came to Ginza to shop for it. How I was surprised at the crowds of people. How I had found it impossible to choose something from among so many things in so many shops. How the veteran department store saleswoman, Kijima-san, had reached out and offered me advice. How I decided that I would send some tea because the sample I'd been given was so delicious. How Kijima-san suggested I include a letter. How she drew me a map and I came to Shihodo to buy stationery. How Ken Takarada-san (what a perfect name for the manager of a venerable stationery shop) was so kind to me. How I was taking advantage of that kindness to write this letter on the first floor of the shop . . .

'It's like a journal entry,' I grumbled to myself with a wince. Then I wrote, *There are lots of friendly people in Tokyo, so you don't have to worry.*

Finishing writing was a relief, and I stretched hard from where I sat on the chair. When I lowered my arms, the fountain pen box fell from the desk.

I leaped out of the chair and crouched down in a hurry.

Letters from the Ginza Shihodo Stationery Shop

The inner cushioning had been knocked out of the box, and next to it was a little folded-up piece of paper. I gathered everything up and sat back down at the desk. The piece of paper had Natsuko-san's unique handwriting on it.

Dear Rin,

I can't express this emotion to you right now, so I'll tuck it in here for later.
Rin, I'm so happy you were born.
I'm not sure how much longer we'll be able to be together.
After all, I'm fifty years older than you.
If I could have my wish, I'd want to be by your side always and see everything you do.
I wonder what kind of grown-up you'll be. I wonder what kind of job you'll get.
I'm also curious to see what kind of person you'll fall in love with. I'm nervous you'll be tricked by someone with bad intentions.
Because you're so kind.
But I know that getting involved in your business would be a bother.
So please go on and spread your wings wide.
And always remain dignified.
But until you grow up, please stay a little longer with me.

Natsuko

I wonder how long it was. I couldn't stop crying. After rereading the note about five times, I paused. If I didn't stop there, I would

Fountain Pen

have kept reading it over and over forever. I wiped my face with the towel, carefully folded up Natsuko-san's letter, and put it back under the cushion in the pen box. Then I ripped up the final draft of the letter I had just finished and threw it away.

I rose from the chair and looked at the Ginza sky dyed red by the setting sun. After taking three deep breaths to calm down, I picked up my fountain pen again and confronted a blank piece of stationery.

I completely ignored my rough draft and yielded the motions of my pen to the swaying of my heart. I put into words the gratitude I'd missed so many chances to convey, of course, and I also told her how I felt about her. Strangely, I was able to write things I couldn't imagine myself saying aloud. Natsuko-san must have cast some magic on the Montblanc.

The next thing I knew, I had filled seven sheets of stationery. My letter ended like this:

> *It's a bit embarrassing to say as a working adult, but . . .*
> *if I could, I would want to rush straight home to you.*
>
> *I would want to cry until I was worn out and then fill my belly with your tasty cooking.*
>
> *But I'm sure you wouldn't allow me to abandon my work like that.*
>
> *So I'll stick it out a little longer.*
>
> *You might be lonely, too, but please hold on for a little longer.*
>
> *I'm planning to take time off for Obon. So please wait until then.*
>
> *I'll keep writing to you – with the Montblanc you gave me.*
>
> *Talk to you soon.*

Letters from the Ginza Shihodo Stationery Shop

Phew. Just as I heaved a big sigh, a voice called out from behind me.

'Were you able to write something?'

'Yes, I'm finally done. Oh, thank you for the tea and snack. It was all very good.'

Takarada-san said, 'Please don't mention it,' with a bashful gesture.

'Oh, for the front of the envelope, what should I write? I probably don't need to write an address since it'll be packed in with the tea...'

'Right. I think writing the person's name is a good idea. And you can put your name on the back.' Takarada-san took a book out of a drawer and said, 'There's an example here,' as he opened it and set it in front of me.

I copied the example and wrote *Natsuko Nitta-sama* on the front and *Rin* on the back.

Then I folded the sheets of stationery into thirds, slipped them into the envelope, glued it shut, and wrote the sealing character, *shime*.

'Phew.' I sighed in spite of myself.

Takarada-san held out a paper Shihodo bag with a little smile. 'Keep it in here till you give it to Kijima-san so it doesn't get dirty.'

Before now, I'm sure I would have only been able to apologise for making him go out of his way. But before I knew it, I had stood up and said, 'Th-thank you!' with a bow. Even I was surprised.

'Oh, none of that. I'm happy to be of service. Now, you'd better get going to Matsukiya. One final errand!'

Once I had packed my things on the desk into my backpack, Takarada-san handed me a piece of paper folded into a knot.

Fountain Pen

'Err, I realise this will require some effort on your part, but could I ask you to give this to Kijima-san?'

'What is it?'

'Well, just a little thank-you note.'

On the knot, it said *To Kijima-sama* and on the reverse side it said, *Ken. People in Ginza are on a whole other level*, I thought.

'OK, I'll make sure to deliver it.'

I put the note in the same bag as my letter. Somehow I felt like I'd been entrusted with an important mission.

I had managed to reach Shihodo without getting lost, and the way back to Matsukiya was even easier, so it took less than half the time. When I rode the escalator down to the basement, Kijima-san stood up as if she had been waiting for me.

'Welcome back!'

'Sorry I took so long.' It felt just like talking to Natsuko-san. I couldn't help but chuckle. 'I didn't mean to keep you waiting. Here's the letter.' I took it out of my backpack and handed it to her. I was surprised to see her accept it with both hands, her head bowed in reverence.

'I'll take care of it from here.'

The trustworthy look on her face made her beautiful. As I was admiring her in spite of myself, I remembered the note from Takarada-san.

'Oh, and this is from the man at Shihodo,' I said, handing her the paper knot.

She exclaimed, 'Wow, Ken-chan has learned some charming tricks, hasn't he?' and undid the knot on the spot.

'What does it say?'

'Hey now, it might be a love letter, so don't be nosy. Just kidding!

Letters from the Ginza Shihodo Stationery Shop

"Thank you for introducing such a lovely customer. We've gotten a number of new postcard designs in, so please stop by soon. Sincerely looking forward to seeing you." Couldn't he write something a bit more amorous? But for Ken-chan, I suppose that was pretty good.'

As she chuckled warmly, I straightened up and bowed to her. 'Thank you so much for all your help.'

She looked a bit surprised, but then bowed neatly with a straight back. 'It was nothing. Thank *you*.'

I managed to say thank you the moment I thought it. Maybe it's not a big deal, but for me, it might have been the greatest achievement of the day.

* * *

Ginza in the rain as a subject of a Shin-hanga print is picturesque, but for locations without an arcade or underground walkway, rain definitely causes foot traffic to wane.

Having finished his prep to open up the shop, the manager of Shihodo Stationery, Ken Takarada, put an umbrella stand next to the door. The wet, new leaves of the willow tree were a pleasant sight, and the vermilion of the old postbox gleamed. After watching the road with its sparse pedestrians for a few moments, Ken went back inside.

As he was about to close the glass double doors, a young customer showed up. Ken held open a door and softly welcomed him. 'Irasshaimase.'

'Do you remember me?' The young customer grinned mischievously as he neatly folded up his umbrella and stuck it into the stand.

'Of course, Nitta-sama. Welcome.'

Fountain Pen

'Wow, you even remember my name.' Nitta was unable to conceal his surprise.

As he welcomed him in, Ken added, 'Yes, there's no way I could forget how earnestly you composed that letter.'

Nitta scratched his head somewhat bashfully. 'You really helped me out the other day. My grandmother wrote back right away. Reading her reply, it was clear she was happy. It's as though exchanging these letters lifted something that had been lying heavy between us.'

'Well! That's wonderful news.'

'Also, I've been using the Montblanc at work, and I get the feeling that whenever I feel unsure about something, the pen gives me a nudge. Before, I was always shy and unable to say what needed to be said, but recently, bit by bit, I've been learning to assert myself more.'

'Oh? Is that right?' Ken murmured in surprise.

'So I came because I'd like to write an update to my grandmother. I still have some stationery and envelopes from last time, but I'd like to try something different. Do you have a recommendation? And would it be all right if I borrow the desk upstairs again?'

'Yes, of course,' Ken replied with a warm smile, and Nitta followed him to the back of the sales floor.

The rain was unlucky. But in one corner of Ginza, Tokyo, at Shihodo Stationery, a soft, warm atmosphere seemed to indicate there was good weather ahead.

Organiser

I thought I'd upped the drinking pace quite a bit even just at the club, but I still got roped into going out afterwards. By the time I'd put the customer into a taxi, it was after 3 a.m.

After getting home and taking a shower, I should have gone straight to my desk – sitting down for 'a moment' on the couch was my mistake. The next thing I knew, I could see the morning sun coming through the lace curtains. *How long have I been asleep?*

I rushed into the dining room and opened the laptop I keep on the table. As expected, my inbox was full of emails. Most of them were questions and confirmations along the lines of, 'About the layout', 'Choosing your logo', 'Hiring male staff' and the like.

Though there were many unread messages, one subject line in particular jumped out at me.

'Please respond by tomorrow'.

One look at the sender and I didn't even have to read the message to know what it was about.

Even I knew I had to hurry up. I just wasn't sure what to do. Feeling stuck, I searched around on the web even though I knew it wouldn't help, but all the advice was too general. None of it seemed even a tiny bit useful for my current situation.

In the first place, I didn't have the right equipment. I'd heard

Letters from the Ginza Shihodo Stationery Shop

that back in the day, a hostess who wasn't an enthusiastic letter writer couldn't get a job, but these days a smartphone did the trick. On the contrary, whether you sent it to their home or their place of work, a letter would only be annoying; hardly any customers would appreciate something like that.

'. . . So I guess the first step is a shopping trip,' I said aloud without really meaning to.

I approached everything, whether hobbies or work, via form. If I don't have the right tools or apparel, I can't get motivated. I think a lot of that is influence from Fumi-mama.

Having made one decision, my mood lifted a bit. I put beans in the coffee maker and bread in the toaster. I lined up some bacon in the frying pan, cracked an egg into it, and julienned some lettuce. Add some orange juice and it's a breakfast of champions.

Strictly observing Fumi-mama's teachings, I skimmed the five national newspapers and two sports papers I'd been subscribed to for years while I ate and then changed into a plain pantsuit. After throwing on a modest makeup look, I thought ahead to bringing my purchases home and chose a large-ish tote bag, then chucked my wallet, phone and trusty Filofax organiser into it.

I checked my reflection in the mirror by the door and selected a pair of low heels. Recently, I've been trying to use trains and buses for travel as much as possible outside of commuting to and from the club. I'm too busy to go to the gym as much as I'd like, so walking even short distances counts as precious exercise to me.

From my room to Ginza, it takes less than thirty minutes in a taxi, but by train, counting the walking time and then two transfers and whatnot, it takes fifty minutes. And unlike in 7-chome

Organiser

or 8-chome, I wasn't very familiar with the area around my destination this time.

Walking the alleyways using the map on my phone as my guide, it didn't take long to find the landmark, a cylindrical postbox. That made me so happy, I picked up my pace as I approached the entrance. But then ...

CLOSED TODAY

It was written clearly in dark brush strokes on the wooden sign hanging on the inside of the glass door. Confused, I checked the website I'd only just been looking at. It plainly stated, 'Closed Wednesday'. On top of that, the opening hours were 10 a.m. to 7 p.m. It was just a little past 9 a.m. on a Wednesday. Not only did I not see anyone inside, the lights weren't even on.

'... Way to go, me.'

I have a habit of getting ahead of myself.

'May I help you?'

I jumped at the sudden voice behind me. I turned around to find a man wearing a grey polo and beige chinos who must have been in his mid-thirties. Perhaps my alarm had startled him? His mouth was hanging nervously open.

'Err, sorry to catch you off guard. It's just that I came here only to find that the shop's closed, so I'm at my wit's end.'

'My humble apologies, but we're closed on Wednesdays.'

He bowed low as if he really was sorry.

'Ah, do you ... work here?'

I thought it might be rude, but I had to ask.

'I do ...'

'Um! I'm terribly sorry to bother you on your day off, but I really need to write a resignation request today. I'd like you to recommend some paper and envelopes that wouldn't be strange

Letters from the Ginza Shihodo Stationery Shop

to use for such a purpose. I realise you're closed, but do you think there's any way you could possibly help me?'

The man cocked his head and seemed to consider it for a moment before nodding succinctly. 'Very well, follow me. You came all the way here, and it seems like your circumstances must be complicated, so I couldn't just do nothing,' he said and led the way.

I followed him around the back to find an old wooden gate that didn't really go with the smart front of the shop. There was a small sign that said SHIHODO SERVICE ENTRANCE and a nameplate that said TAKARADA. *So this must be Takarada-san.*

I followed Takarada-san through the gate and closed the wooden door behind me.

'This way, please.'

He slid the door open. Inside was an earthen floor and two doors on either side. He opened the right-hand door and invited me in. 'It's this way.' It was the shop's sales floor.

'Thank you.'

As I walked onto the floor, Takarada-san used a hand behind his back to shut the door. The empty shop was, it goes without saying, silent, and it looked like the products were asleep on their shelves. In part because it was still relatively early in the morning, there wasn't much light coming in through the windows facing the street, and with the lights off, the shop felt somehow lonely in its darkness.

It's the total opposite of the 'shop' where I work. During business hours, we have warm lighting, more dim than bright. But when we're not open, there's intense, white LED lighting – more often than not, it's easy to find the earring or cufflink we had no hope of locating at the time it was lost.

Organiser

'OK, right this way.'

Takarada-san extended an arm to guide me towards shelves lined with products, and past that was a staircase. At the top of the dimly lit stairs I could see the slightly brighter first floor.

'I'm sorry to make you climb the stairs, but please go to the first floor. If we talk down here, other customers might get the mistaken impression the shop is open.' He directed me towards the stairs with a 'Go ahead.'

Though it wasn't that much higher up, the first floor was filled with light. On the right was a raised tatami area, and the entire wall on the other side of the room was fitted with drawers and sliding-door cabinets. It looked just like the chest of medicine drawers I'd seen at a Chinese medicine store in Taiwan.

In the centre of the room were six long worktables set up in a rectangle. They resembled desks you might see in an office, but wider and longer with tops of sturdy plywood and thick aprons and legs. The rubber casters were the kind you see on hand trolleys, with big metal stoppers. They felt kind of like stage props.

There was a large desk beside the window on the left at the back of the room. It gave off a strong air of its times and stood out in the bright, white light of the room.

'All right, here you are.'

Takarada-san pulled out a chair at one of the worktables in the centre of the room.

'Thank you.' I took the seat as offered. Right away, I set my tote bag on the floor, took out my organiser and Cross ballpoint pen and put them on the table. I didn't really think I would need to take notes, but whether by habit or tic, whenever I sit down at a table, I unconsciously unpack my stuff.

'You have a pretty voice. And the intonation of your "thank

you" is so pleasant. You must have rehearsed it quite a bit,' he said with a smile before adding, 'One moment, please.'

Then he went over to the drawers in the wall, took out several types of paper and envelopes, and laid them out in front of me.

'These are simple designs that can be used for any purpose. I do think they're perhaps overly plain, but for a resignation request, that may be best . . . Err, not to pry, but you're sure it's a resignation request and not a resignation notification?'

'Hm? Oh, yes, it's a request. But is there a difference between the two?'

Takarada-san gave a small nod.

'A request is for floating the idea that you'd like to resign. A notification is for formally stating your intentions in writing to someone from whom you've already received informal consent.'

'. . . Huh, I didn't know that.'

'So . . . you haven't told your boss that you want to quit yet? Most people express their wish to leave verbally, so I think it's pretty rare to write or submit a resignation request or letter . . .'

I wasn't sure how to respond. '. . . Well, I want to say it, but I just can't . . . So I thought I'd try submitting a written request.'

'Hrrm,' groaned Takarada-san, and he fell silent for a time. 'This may be presumptuous, but I feel like there must be more going on. Would you mind telling me about your circumstances? I feel like we must have met for a reason. I'd like to help you come up with a solution.'

'I see . . . I'm not putting you out . . . ?'

Takarada-san shook his head. 'No. After all, I both live and work here. And I don't have any set plans today – to the point that I was even thinking I might refresh the product display this afternoon. So you can rest easy about that.'

Organiser

Upon replying, he put away the stationery he'd been showing me.

'Th-then if I'm not intruding . . .' I stood up and bowed instinctively.

'None of that! It can't be good luck for me to make a customer feel that way!' he said, flustered. Then he continued. 'Err, before we begin . . . may I make some tea?'

'Tea? Of course, please do. I'm imposing after all, so it wouldn't be my place to stop you.'

He nodded deeply, seeming relieved. 'Then please wait a moment and I'll be right back.'

With that, he disappeared through the door.

A sigh slipped out. The spine I'd been holding so straight went slack and I leaned back in my chair. The lack of sleep made it hard for me to concentrate.

I picked up my planner, put a finger on the To-do index, and flipped it open. Along with *'seal registration'*, *'proof of residence'*, *'club* and *opening announcement draft'* was *'resignation request'*. Before those words was a red star and I'd emphasised it further with a wavy line beneath. The moment I saw it, I emitted another sigh.

As I was staring into space, there came the abrupt sound of the door opening. I hurriedly straightened up. If Fumi-mama could have seen me just now, she would have given me a royal scolding.

'The issue isn't whether someone is watching or not. Create another "you" inside yourself to observe you objectively. You can never fool yourself, no matter what.'

I'm sure that's what she would say. Even I know I still lack polish . . . I thought. Maybe what I was trying to do was reckless after all.

Letters from the Ginza Shihodo Stationery Shop

'Sorry to have kept you waiting.' Takarada-san reappeared carrying a tray. After setting it on the table, he took out a card holder, removed a card, and offered it to me. 'Apologies for the delayed introduction. Ken Takarada of Shihodo Stationery, at your service.'

At such a formal introduction, it was my turn to be flustered. I thrust a hand into my bag, but because I'd simply thrown some things into it as I was rushing out, I didn't have my cards. *Agh!* I thought, but keeping a straight face, I reached for the spare I kept in the card pocket of my organiser.

'I'm Yuri from Club Fumi.'

'By "club" do you mean one of those high-class . . . you know?'

'Yes, that's right.'

'The club where you can enjoy drinks with refined women, not the club you dance at, right?'

I had to laugh. Maybe it was just the image I got, but I never would have expected to hear this guy talk about dance clubs or say the word with such a slangy vibe.

'Sorry, I derailed the conversation,' he apologised.

'Not at all. The club where I work is one of Ginza's finest. The owner, Fumi-mama, opened it in the year of the previous Tokyo Olympics, so its history spans over half a century.'

Ken-san emitted a short 'Ahh', and said, 'It's a bit embarrassing to admit, but though I've lived in Ginza for many years, I've never visited one. Still, even I've heard of Club Fumi. It often gets covered in magazine write-ups on Ginza and when clubs get featured on TV, right?'

He paid close attention to what I was saying as he put tea leaves into a teapot.

'Yes, Fumi-mama accepts interview requests if she thinks it

will help improve working conditions for people in Ginza's bar and restaurant scene. That said, I don't think she's ever let a camera in the club. She always takes interviews in her office.'

As we spoke, Ken-san poured the tea into a tea bowl and cup. He went back and forth between the two, pouring a little bit at a time to ensure that the strength was balanced. He was sitting at a little bit of a distance, but the lovely smell of the tea wafted over to me. I was surprised that a single pot could produce a scent so rich it could fill the room.

'Here you go,' he offered the saucer with both hands.

Without thinking, I bowed my head in gratitude and said '*Chōdai itashimasu.*' It felt just like a tea ceremony. Though it didn't seem proper, I immediately lifted the tea bowl off the tray.

Around the time the bowl approached my chin, the scent tickled my nose. No, far from a tickle, it was a direct assault. I blew gently and took a sip. The tea that slipped between my lips swirled once around my mouth before running down my throat. It tasted sweet with a strong *umami* flavour, and the scent leaving my nasal passages was even more pleasant.

'Ohh, it's delicious . . .' I murmured in spite of myself.

'I'm glad,' Ken-san said with a little smile. Then he softly added, 'Now then, I'm ready to hear your story if you're ready to tell it.'

I replied with a small nod.

I first met Fumi-mama right after I moved to Tokyo. I had just started working part-time for a flower shop in Ginza by way of an introduction from an older graduate of my high school. My job was delivering flowers to clubs, bars, restaurants and other food and drink establishments. But there were so many little side

Letters from the Ginza Shihodo Stationery Shop

streets in Ginza that I had a hard time finding the addresses listed on the delivery slips. Back then, I didn't have a smartphone, so there was no map app to consult.

That day, too, unable to find the address for the life of me, I was standing on the street at my wit's end with the pocket map I'd borrowed from the shop in one hand and the delivery slip in the other. It had been well over half an hour since I'd left, and the specified delivery time was approaching fast. It was the end of April, so not even that hot, but maybe because I'd been walking, sweat was pouring down my forehead.

'What's wrong?' a voice suddenly called out to me.

'Oh, uh, I-I'm trying to go here . . . Do you know where this place is? I guess it's a tempura restaurant . . .'

I ungraciously thrust the delivery slip out. The woman was wearing an expensive-looking suit and smelled wonderful. I became abruptly conscious of my sweaty body odour.

'Oh, what a coincidence. I'm on my way there right now. Why don't we go together? It's just over there.' Then she said, 'This way,' beckoning me as she set off walking. 'So you work for a flower shop. Part-time?' she asked, glancing back to look at me.

'Yes. I just started last week.'

'Is that right? Well, it'll probably be tough while you're getting used to the area, but you'll get some exercise, you can polish your sense of beauty seeing so many flowers, and you'll be able to learn all sorts of things from the customers you deliver to, so I think it's a great job. Do your best. Here we are! Not far at all, right?'

It really had taken only three minutes to get there.

'Now you can make your delivery.'

'Oh! Um, please go in ahead of me. There's still a little while

Organiser

before the designated delivery time. With your help, I managed to arrive without getting too lost. Ah, sorry, I forgot to say thank you. Thank you!' Flustered, I bowed my head.

The woman laughed merrily and shook her head. 'You're being a bit dramatic, but I'm glad I was able to assist. But hey, you're polite, considerate, genuine . . . That seems rare these days. Perhaps we'll meet again somewhere.'

She began walking away instead of going into the restaurant.

'Err, you don't need to go to the restaurant?'

'Hm? Oh, I've just remembered I have an errand to run. I'll go later. See you.' With those parting words, she went back the way we'd come. Then the owner of the tempura restaurant came out.

'Oh, the florist. Thanks. Were you talking to someone just now?'

'Yes, her. I was lost and she was kind enough to show me the way.'

When I pointed to the woman walking away he murmured, 'Ohh,' and then raised his voice to call out, 'Hello!' Surprised, the woman turned around and gave him a little bow with a wave.

'Who is she?'

'What? You got directions from her without knowing? Well, I suppose it makes sense for someone your age. That's Fumi-mama. She's what you might call the poster lady of a high-class club here in Ginza.'

That day after work, I had the shop wrap a single red rose for me. Usually employees bought fully bloomed flowers that hadn't sold, but I said I would pay the normal price and got them to give me the most perfect, bright red rose they had. For just the one, it cost 1,000 yen.

Letters from the Ginza Shihodo Stationery Shop

With the flower in hand I knocked on the door of Club Fumi. It was 5 p.m. and there weren't any customers yet. Even so, as an eighteen-year-old girl in jeans and sneakers with not so much as a dab of makeup on, I felt wildly out of place; just remembering is enough for me to break into a cold sweat. That's how little foresight I had, but I really wanted to say a proper thank-you.

A man in a dark suit, whom I later learned was the general manager, opened the door. When I said I wanted to see Fumi-mama, he looked a bit surprised, but he directed me to the counter just inside and went to find her.

When Fumi-mama came out, she was wearing a kimono and had her hair neatly styled.

'Oh, the girl from the florist. What can I do for you?'

'Er, um, I just appreciated your help today. So I wanted to thank you . . .'

On one corner of the counter was a large vase filled with flowers, and behind the counter a magnificent arrangement was on display. There was no way I could hand her a single rose – how embarrassing.

'What's that you have in your hand?'

She saw right through me. I awkwardly held out the flower.

'It's for me?'

'Sorry. I got the owner of the tempura restaurant to give me this address. I didn't realise it was such a fancy place . . . Thank you so much for earlier.'

I gave her the rose. Fumi-mama accepted it with both hands and bowed her head low.

'Not at all. Thank *you* for going out of your way to bring me such a lovely rose. Now, have a seat right there.'

At those words, the manager slid a stool out for me.

Organiser

'Oh, I don't want to bother you; I should be going.'

'What are you talking about? This is a club. I can't let someone who came through those doors leave without a drink. Oh, but before that, how old are you?'

When I answered eighteen, she laughed. 'Oh, too bad. I nearly had an excuse to open a bottle of champagne!' To the bartender, she said, 'One deluxe fresh juice, please!' and then, 'Could you put this in the single-flower crystal vase?'

The bartender reverently accepted the rose, and the two of us watched in silence as he placed it in the vase. Meanwhile, another staff member placed a glass of juice in front of me and a flute glass in front of Fumi-mama. The general manager said, 'This seems like a fortunate meeting, so here's a gift from me to celebrate, Fumi-mama,' and poured some champagne.

'Oh, how generous of you! I gratefully accept.'

As if in response, the single-flower vase was gently set between us.

'Hey, do you know the meaning of a single, deep red rose?'

Embarrassingly, I did not. I shook my head.

'It's "love at first sight".'

I must have blushed bright red. But it was true that I'd fallen in love with Fumi-mama at first sight.

'Now, cheers. Oh, come to think of it, I haven't properly introduced myself.' Fumi-mama took the card the general manager offered and gave it to me. 'I'm Fumi, the mama here. Nice to meet you.'

I accepted the card with both hands and gave my name. 'I'm Yuri Kawai.'

'Yuri-chan, huh? Yuri-chan gave me a red rose. It sounds like the beginning of a story. I'm glad it wasn't a single *yuri*, though.'

Letters from the Ginza Shihodo Stationery Shop

'Err, as someone working at a flower shop, I'm ashamed to admit that I don't know the meanings of any flowers . . . What's a single lily?'

The general manager standing by behind her said, 'Excuse my intrusion, but . . . if my memory serves, it's for presenting to a deceased person.'

Flustered, I said, 'Oh, really?!'

Fumi-mama watched the exchange in amusement and added, 'It's true that some people with nasty tongues say I'm either a *yokai* or a ghost, but I'm not about to bite the dust yet!'

The charming way she spoke made me chuckle.

'Hey, how would you like to work here once you turn twenty? Oh, you don't have to respond now. Think it over. In fact, once you're twenty, just pop into the office listed on the back of that business card. You really are so genuine, you've got charm – I like you. Hey, remember this girl, OK?'

The general manager bowed and said, 'Yes, ma'am.'

So it was then I began working at Club Fumi after Golden Week in my junior year of college. That means it's been about ten years. At most clubs, girls can start working at eighteen, but Club Fumi only hires girls over twenty. So I waited for two years. According to Fumi-mama, 'We're a drinking establishment, right? It wouldn't do for a customer to offer a girl a drink and her to say, "Sorry, I can't." Of course, if you don't do well with alcohol, that's a different matter, and there's no need to force yourself, but we can't put our customers in illegal situations.'

She doesn't hire smokers, either – neither hostesses nor male staff. 'You can pair a customer who enjoys a smoke with a girl who doesn't partake, but you can't pair a girl who smokes with a customer who doesn't care for smoking.'

It's sound logic, but apparently there was a time she really struggled to hire people. And naturally, if someone started smoking after joining, Fumi-mama, sensitive to scents as she is, would notice right away and confront them sternly: 'You can quit smoking or quit the club – make your choice.' Several hostesses and staff members really did choose to leave for that reason.

The club itself was non-smoking long before the prefectural ordinance changed, so by the time I arrived, there was already a smoking booth. If a customer just had to have a cigarette, we directed them there. Despite being that inconvenient for customers, we were always busy – Club Fumi really is a curious place.

That said, most of the regulars were health-conscious, and there were very few smokers. And the smokers we did have tended to enjoy the fragrance of a cigar or pipe rather than smoke cigarettes. When those customers go into the smoking booth, they don't come out for an hour. I don't know what the smokers gathered in there talk about among themselves, but they sure have fun. It makes me wonder why they pay so much money to go to the club if they're not going to interact with the hostesses.

Well, I went on a tangent, but there were a bunch of other restrictions for student part-timers.

'A student's job is to study. So I'm perfectly happy to have you for a couple of hours a week. And you should be able to still make pretty good money. As long as you don't splurge or get sucked into giving money to some guy, it should be plenty, right?'

Letters from the Ginza Shihodo Stationery Shop

In that way, Fumi-mama made a sharp distinction between student part-timers and full-time hostesses. To this day, students are prohibited from companion commutes or after time.

'Um . . . what are companion commutes and after time?' Ken-san asked me.

'Huh? Oh, right, I suppose you don't know. Companion commuting means getting treated to dinner by a customer before the club opens and then showing up at the club together. Though dinner is paid for, you're acting as a companion outside of working hours, so it's a kind of business activity. After time means going out for drinks with a customer after the club closes. That also counts as business outside working hours.'

'I see . . . You have to be a companion to them even outside the club – sounds like hard work.'

If you're on a companion commute, it means showing up at the restaurant at 6 p.m. And to allow time to get ready, you need to be in Ginza by around 4 p.m., so that would affect your afternoon and early evening classes.

After time means after the club closes, so you'd be with the customer until at least 2 a.m. By the time you get home and do whatever you need to do to get ready for bed, it's dawn. There's no way you'd make it to first period.

As days like that pile up, girls show up for school less and less and eventually drop out. Fumi-mama was strongly against that.

'You've done all the work to be in school, so make sure you graduate. Even if you haven't found the reason for your studies yet, the day will come when you'll be happy you got your degree,' she would say and take special care with the schedules of

Organiser

part-time hostesses. Whenever there were exams or seminars or lab trips, we could always get time off.

Incidentally, if we turned in a copy of our report cards, Fumi-mama would give us allowances out of pocket depending on our results. An S was worth 3,000 yen, an A was 1,000, and Bs and Cs got us nothing. For the failing grades, a D was minus 500 and an F was minus 1,000. So we could get between 10,000 and 20,000 yen – not a significant amount to Fumi-mama, but for part-timers it was extra income, which did boost our motivation.

For working hours, she makes a sharp distinction between part-timers and full-timers, but when it comes to education, she doesn't compromise. Everyone, whether newbie or veteran, is required to attend study sessions.

'Study sessions? Like she invites teachers to the club to give lectures?'

I understood Ken-san's reaction.

'Yes, once a month. All the lecturers are top-class, and they come up with ways to keep us engaged. I actually look forward to them. Hm? The subjects? Well, politics, economics or some scientific topic that has been making the news. And I guess lots of history, too. Mama and the managers put their heads together to plan the curriculum each year.'

'Wow, that's amazing.' Ken-san put a hand to his jaw, tremendously impressed.

'The idea is to make sure we acquire a balance of knowledge so that customers can enjoy chatting with us about this and that. And, in fact, after the lecturer leaves, she says, without fail, "OK, now take everything you just learned and put it away in a drawer in your head – please don't blah blah about it to customers. Don't forget that I'm having you study so that you'll make better conversation companions. Even if a customer says something that contradicts what you've just learned, don't argue with them. Got it?"'

'Hearing that makes me feel even more scared to go to a club,' Ken-san said, heaving a sigh.

'Hmm, that wasn't my intention. But the best hostesses are all good listeners, so I don't think most customers notice. At any rate, Fumi-mama has always encouraged hostesses and other staff members in their learning.'

Yes, Fumi-mama is always watching – she sees even the smallest efforts a hard worker puts in.

About two weeks after I started at Club Fumi, I participated in my first study session. The subject was super computers. As a more humanities-minded student, it was gobbledygook to me. To be honest, I didn't understand a thing, but I wrote down everything the teacher said. I understood so little that most of my notes were in *hiragana* or *katakana* since I didn't know kanji for the unfamiliar words; I could never show them to anyone – too crude. I decided I would at least look up the words that piqued my interest later.

After the lecture ended and the teacher left, Fumi-mama came over to me.

'How admirable of you to take notes!'

I was holding the pen and notebook I'd bought at a 100-yen store on the way to the club.

'We have study sessions once a month, so please make it a habit. I'm sure the lecturers will see that serious "I'm listening with all my might!" face as you write in your notebook.'

I was happy to receive her praise.

Organiser

'But that pen and notebook are out of the question. A top-class hostess only surrounds herself with top-class things. Oh, but the highest quality doesn't always mean a high price, so don't misunderstand. No matter how expensive something is, an inferior product will never be called top class.'

The,n with a 'Keep up the good work,' she walked away. I was happy that she spoke to me, but the content of her message was challenging.

On my way home that day, I took a bit of a detour to look at the windows of the department stores. I thought if I examined the dazzling displays, I'd get an idea of what it meant to be top class. But I came away without a single clue.

The next day when I went to work, there was a package in my locker tied with a bow. Inside, I found a notebook along with a sheet of stationery with what looked like Fumi-mama's writing on it.

A reward for your efforts yesterday. Keep it up!

It was a magnificent notebook with a cover made of leather or something similar. According to the label on the inside, it was a Filofax Notebook Classic. Next to the notebook was a gold pen. The warranty said 'Cross Classic Century 14-Karat Gold-Filled Ballpoint Pen N1502'.

Near the pen's grip, an engraving in a modestly sized hand-written font said 'Yuri'.

Nobody had ever given me any kind of reward before. It was so unexpected, I felt a little strange, but at the same time I was so incredibly happy.

That day I found time alone in an elevator with Fumi-mama

after seeing off a customer and thanked her. She responded with a little smile, 'You're welcome,' and gave me a pat on the shoulder.

When I got home that night I copied the notes from the 100-yen-store notebook into the new one. The slight heft of the Cross pen allowed the ball at the tip to roll comfortably, so writing was a breeze. Since then I've been taking study session notes with the Filofax notebook and Cross pen Fumi-mama gave me. Of course, I used up the notebook's pages long ago, so I've continued buying the same kind – I'm on my fifth.

'I see, so that's why your organiser is also Filofax, huh?'

Though he was seated at a bit of a distance, Ken-san had guessed the brand of my organiser. I suppose I'd expect nothing less from the manager of a venerable stationery shop.

'Oh, no. Actually, Fumi-mama gave me this, too – on a different occasion.'

'I'm even more interested in meeting her, now. Giving stationery and writing utensils as presents is actually quite difficult. Everyone has their own preferences when it comes to appearance – design, colours, size – and the feel of both pens or paper differs so much between products. Unless you know the person you're buying for really well, it's hard to choose something they'll like.'

'Do you think so . . . ? Well, Fumi-mama is a serial giver; she's constantly giving little presents not only to me but to all the hostesses and staff members. Sometimes they come on your birthday or the day you started at the club, but other times you'll think, "Why today?" A day when you're feeling down – or on the contrary, feeling up . . .'

Ken-san murmured, 'Hmm . . . That's amazing. She sounds

so motherly.' And that's the truth: Fumi-mama is the mother of everyone who works at the club.

Fumi-mama encouraged hostesses and staff to expand their learning beyond the study sessions at the club. Partially as a result of that stance, not only the general manager, but some of the other managers, too, have gone for their sommelier's licence. Among the bartenders are a few who are easily talented enough to work at a standard bar without hostesses and have even won prizes for their skills at the international level. Incidentally, Club Fumi employs bartenders behind the counter and floor staff outside it.

Naturally, Fumi-mama encouraged her staff to acquire sommelier licences and bartending techniques – knowledge and skills that related directly to the club's business – but that wasn't all; she urged people behind the counter to get cook or nutritionist licences and those on the floor to get bookkeeping or labour management licences. Sometimes she even offered 'scholarships' for vocational school or correspondence course tuition.

'I'd like you to work here forever, but if you marry and your family grows, or due to whatever life brings, you might need to change your work situation, right? If you work at night, you'll always be on the opposite schedule from your family, so you might want to switch to a daytime job. When that day comes, "I was working at Club Fumi" alone won't get you anywhere. That's why it's important to get the licences that will back you up when you talk about the knowledge and experience you gained. And you can't pass the tests without going back and getting the fundamentals down, so it's worth getting the licence to iron out any idiosyncrasies you might have, too.'

Letters from the Ginza Shihodo Stationery Shop

I remember her saying that to me once. Oh, and one other thing:

'Feeling like you need to study means you'll have less time to play around, right? It's much better than resorting to gambling to kill time or getting hooked on some weird hobby.'

She said it with a smile. I'm not sure how much was how she really felt and how much was to conceal her own self-consciousness.

At any rate, Fumi-mama is a worrier so she's always looking out for her hostesses and staff. When she heard a couple of brothers on staff had exams coming up, she went out of her way to Yushima Tenjin and brought back academic luck charms, and whenever a girl says she has a headache, she comes flying over with the first-aid box. She really is everyone's 'mama'.

Of course, Fumi-mama is my Tokyo mother, too. I talk to her about everything from school to friends, to boyfriends, and she's always cared about me. A twenty-year-old girl from the countryside is a bundle of ignorance, so if I hadn't met Fumi-mama, I don't think I'd be who I am today.

'They say there's no bigger influence on your life than the people you meet along the way,' said Ken-san with a deep nod.

'So true . . .' I said before continuing my story.

Thanks to being taken under Fumi-mama's wing like that, I reached the point where my graduation was secure and it was time to start exploring full-time employment options. I had intended to graduate and work full-time as a hostess at Club Fumi. But Fumi-mama's response was blunt.

'You should experience what it's like to be a normal

Organiser

working adult. Which industry doesn't matter, just join as strait-laced a company as you can find – if possible, a listed one because they'll spend time and money on employee education. Work there for three years. Then if you still want to come back, I'll hire you.'

Since I had expected to be hired full-time upon graduation, this was a bit disappointing. But I think that it was another example of Fumi-mama's kindness.

'If you meet someone nice at the office or a client's office, get married. It's better if you don't have to come back here . . .' she'd said, looking a little sad.

In the end, I chose a company that manufactured equipment for processing metal. When I reported to Fumi-mama about the informal offer, she pulled out *Kaisha Shikiho* and looked the company up. After five minutes skimming the data on it in the magazine, she nodded deeply.

'That should be a good choice. It's nothing fancy, but it seems to have a stable track record. And I haven't heard any rumours about the executives listed here carousing in Ginza. I'm sure this place is fine.'

These days plenty of people prefer cabaret bars in Roppongi or the exclusive lounges of the Azabu area, so just because someone's name doesn't come up in Ginza doesn't mean they aren't out there messing around, but I didn't say anything.

One day in March right after my graduation ceremony, Fumi-mama called me into her office. In addition to Club Fumi, she runs a wine bar, an Italian restaurant, a cafe and other businesses, so she's also the CEO of her management company, Letterbox Ltd.

The office is in an old mixed-use building on the border

between 7- and 8-chome, a clean but simple room. When I arrived five minutes before the specified time, I found Fumi-mama in a chic suit – like she'd been wearing the first time I met her – along with sunglasses; she seemed like a completely different person from the one she was at the club.

The moment we met she presented me with a 'congratulations on your full-time employment' envelope decorated with paper strings, as well as an origami *noshi* in the corner and a gift-wrapped box.

'It's not much, but congratulations.'

When I opened the envelope later, I found 200,000 yen inside. It was way too much to give to a part-time hostess.

'Buy three pairs of good shoes. Take good care of them so that anyone who sees your feet sees them looking good. I've been keeping an eye on my customers' feet all these years, so I know what I'm talking about. Nobody with properly polished shoes is third-rate or below.'

The box had a Filofax organiser in it.

'New hires who studied humanities generally get assigned to the sales team – unless they have some really special talent. Ultimately, sales is all about whether you can get important clients to like you or not. Of course, you work hard and refuse to let anyone beat you, so I don't have to worry, but you know.'

The black leather, A5-size organiser had 'Yuri' embossed in gold leaf in the upper right-hand corner.

'I get lots of salespeople here, too, some great, others not so much. But half of everything is based on first impressions, and the other half is decided during the small talk we exchange while trading business cards. And I always check their organiser or notebook. I can tell if someone is trustworthy based on what

Organiser

they take notes with. The worst are the people who take notes on sales sheets they brought with them or the margins of a catalogue. None of those people ever follow through on what we discuss.'

Her concern for me extends even to my new job? And she got me an organiser? The thought made my heart full. Tears spilled onto the pretty leather cover.

'Ahh, that'll leave a mark! Good grief. Leather is durable, but it doesn't do well with water. Oh, you can find refills for the inside at any big stationery store or online. Run it ragged and get promoted!'

With that, she sent me on my way.

As Fumi-mama expected, I was assigned to the sales team. I was attached to Ota Ward and tasked with going around to all the small to medium-sized factories there.

All the companies I dealt with were headed up by presidents who were very particular and said things like, 'We supply parts for NASA, you know' and 'If we stopped developing new parts, smartphone evolution would be over!' and they had lots of annoying requests, but it did make the job interesting.

Curiously, it was always at the more obsessive companies that employees endearingly called their president *Oyajisan*, and his wife, who would be in charge of accounting or some such task, *Okamisan*.

Even at small to mid-sized companies, the larger ones could have over a hundred employees, but Oyajisan would show up before everyone else and wipe everything down while greeting each worker as they arrived, and Okamisan would serve everyone tea – they really treated employees like family. Yes, just like at Club Fumi. For that reason, and others, I enjoyed visiting our favourite clients.

Letters from the Ginza Shihodo Stationery Shop

The only knowledge I had about my own company's products was what I had learned during training, and I didn't know a thing about our clients, so everywhere I went I furiously took notes in the Filofax organiser Fumi-mama gave me. I made a separate tab for each client, took notes on our discussions each time I visited, and made sure to follow through on whatever I agreed to.

One day, I was visiting a client who hadn't put in an order in a while, and the okamisan – that is, the president's wife – took the catalogue I handed her and said, with genuine emotion, 'I really admire you, Kawai-san.'

I had no idea what she was talking about, so I'm sure a flock of question marks were flying over my head. Maybe there was something funny about the confused look on my face. She cracked up and said, 'You look like you don't understand what you're being complimented for. The thing is, when I say, "Please bring a catalogue with you the next time we meet," it's only about one in ten people who actually do it. Nowadays you can download a PDF from the website, so I get it, but . . . I'm happy that you remembered my request.'

With that she said, 'Here you go,' and offered me tea for the first time.

'You're always taking notes in that big planner of yours, aren't you? The president always says, "She takes notes to judge everyone! You'll get laughed at if you say anything stupid," but I like how hard you work. It's clear you'll never miss a single word we say!'

At the time, my sales record wasn't really improving, so her words made me so happy I cried.

*

Organiser

'It's pretty rare for a gift to actually be useful to the person who receives it . . .' said Ken-san.

'. . . I suppose. I mentioned it to Fumi-mama once and she said, "It's because you're a devoted note-taker – nothing to do with the tool." Of course, maybe that was just to cover up her self-consciousness.'

'Did you keep in touch with her after you started working?'

'Yes, less on my side than on hers. She contacted me often, like a mother concerned for her freshly moved-out daughter.'

Fumi-mama did LINE and call often, asking things like, 'Are you eating properly?' or 'It sure got chilly fast. You didn't catch a cold, did you?' Just short messages, but I was happy to receive them because I could see she hadn't forgotten about me.

Sometimes she sent seasonal fruit, juice or jelly with a little note that said, 'A customer gave me a bunch, so here's some for you.' Living alone, it wasn't always convenient to buy fruit, so I appreciated it. She said they were gifts from someone else, but I'm pretty sure she actually bought them especially for me.

Of course, customers really do give you things. The most common is fish. When customers who like to fish get a good haul, they show up with Styrofoam containers chock-full of horse mackerel, sillago or whatnot.

On these days, one of the bartenders who used to work as a high-class Japanese cuisine cook would clean them and fry them up, offering them to customers as a free treat and sending any leftovers home with hostesses and staff.

And if it seemed like there would still be extras, I'd sometimes get a phone call.

'Yuri-chan, can you stop by the club?'

Letters from the Ginza Shihodo Stationery Shop

I'd always arrive to delicious fish. They cooked the fried horse mackerel or sillago tempura so it would be ready just as I walked in, and it tasted out of this world. There would even be rice and miso soup . . . 'You look like my daughter home for a visit,' one of the old regulars would tease.

Between this and that, the three years of my company employment flew by. In January of the third year, I made an appointment at Fumi-mama's office and went to see her.

Once shown to the sitting room, I took out my Filofax and opened it to the Q&A page I'd prepped. I'd read my notes so many times I had them all memorised.

When Fumi-mama came into the room, her eyes landed on the organiser in my lap.

'Can I see that for a minute? Don't worry, I won't read what you've written.'

I closed the Filofax and handed it over. She took it carefully with both hands and stroked the cover. I had meant to take good care of it, but there were nonetheless little nicks here and there. She gently stroked each one as if to say, 'Nice work.'

'OK, thank you. I can tell you've been working hard, Yuri-chan.' Then she returned it to me. 'You've been using the Cross pen, too, I see.'

From there we both trailed off into a period of silence. It lasted only a short while, probably not even three minutes, but it felt incredibly long.

'So, are you really coming back? Of course, it'd be my pleasure, and speaking as a manager, you're an attractive hire – since you're experienced and also have a lot of potential. I can't see any reason not to sign you up, but . . . Three years may seem long, but they're over so quickly. You didn't find anyone special?'

Organiser

When I said, 'There aren't many people cooler than you, Fumi-mama,' she heaved a sigh and said, 'Then I suppose you're hired!' offering her hand for a shake.

I still remember clearly the feel of her hand in mine.

Ken-san, fully committed to his role as listener – nodding at times or asking the meaning of words he didn't know – murmured, 'The more I hear, the more I want to meet Fumi-mama.' Really, I would have liked to say, 'By all means! Stop by any time!' but all I could do was avert my gaze in silence.

'Ah . . . So that's what the resignation request is for.'

I replied with a nod and continued my story.

Upon returning to the club, I achieved some success and was eventually able to contribute to its profits. At any rate, every day was so much fun, I felt like I wanted to stay at Club Fumi forever. Of course I also made a ton of mistakes, and got told off plenty of times by Fumi-mama.

But no matter how much she reprimanded me, I never felt bad – because I could tell from her every word that she loved me. I don't really even understand, but it's somehow different from getting scolded by a teacher at school or my boss at my previous job. I can't quite understand, but maybe it's similar to the way a mother scolds a child by saying, 'You'll get hurt if you go running into the street like that!' Like she's so worried I'll find myself in trouble that she ends up lecturing me.

And Fumi-mama wasn't only hard on the hostesses and other staff members. She was also stern with customers who let themselves go a little too wild.

There was this one customer who had started showing up

Letters from the Ginza Shihodo Stationery Shop

soon after I had left. He ran a company that developed smartphone apps, or something. Living the high life, he always spent a significant amount when he came in, but once under the influence, his tone grew violent.

One day soon after I'd started working full-time, he came in alone following dinner with a client and quite a few drinks at the wine bar they'd gone to after that. He seemed pretty drunk already, and he ignored Fumi-mama's disapproval and began teasing this girl he'd met for the first time – me. He was really grilling me about every little thing, where I'd gone to school, my previous job and so on – he wouldn't let up.

Fumi-mama tried to swap in a veteran to spare me, but he said, 'No, no, I like this one. She's interesting,' and wouldn't let me go.

Finally, he said, 'Aren't you embarrassed to be a hostess in Ginza with those looks?'

'What are you talking about?! We only have beautiful women at this club!' Fumi-mama defended me, but it seemed to irk the guy, and he continued drinking at quite a pace.

A little later, Fumi-mama got up to see some customers out, and the guy came at me with, 'Hey, do your parents know their daughter works at a place like this? I bet they think you still work at your strait-laced company job.'

My parents divorced when I was in junior high, but I was on good terms with both of them and had kept in touch since moving to Tokyo. I'd told them when I started working at the club part-time and when I quit my job to go back. So I answered the man with a mild, 'My parents know, so everything's fine.'

'Making their daughter go to work in Ginza – what are they doing with all the money you make? It's disgusting.'

Organiser

I'm sure my anger must have shown on my face. Now I'd be able to shoot back a glib, 'Right? I'm such a dutiful child!' but back then I had just come back to the club and didn't have the composure.

'What's that look for?' In the next instant, he threw the contents of his glass in my face. The other hostesses screamed, and one of the male staff members came rushing over. The floor manager appeared immediately and asked the customer if something had offended him.

'This chick was glaring at me with that sulky face, so I washed it for her, that's all!' The manager was just as fed up with the shouting customer as the rest of us. That was when Fumi-mama returned.

'I gather you were disappointed with our hospitality. My apologies.' Then she bowed deeply. Seeming satisfied, the customer repositioned himself on the sofa.

'But throwing a drink in someone's face is violence. If I decided to report you, you'd be arrested for assault. You're well aware of that, I'm sure?'

'Ah, err, I mean, my hand just slipped—'

'You're old enough not to make pathetic excuses like that! How about you just admit what you did?'

Her defiance seemed to sober him up all at once, and he froze.

Fumi-mama exhaled deeply and said in her usual calm tone, 'Also, my employees are family to me. Anyone abusing them is no customer of mine. Kindly take your leave. And please don't come back. Oh, and you don't need to pay for today.'

'Please see him outside,' she said to the staff, and two members escorted him out and sent him on his way.

Letters from the Ginza Shihodo Stationery Shop

Fumi-mama went around to each table to apologise for the disturbance, offering fruit and drinks on the house. I cleaned up quick with wet wipes and a towel before accompanying Fumi-mama as she requested.

At each table, we were met with kind remarks.

'That was rough. I'm impressed you could put up with it.'

And then Fumi-mama would say, 'Oh, you overheard?'

'Well, yeah, he was yelling.'

'If you could hear, you should have rescued her!'

'I was thinking it was about time to jump in, and then he splashed her. Just as I was like "That's enough," rolling up my sleeves, you came back, so I missed my chance.'

'Lies! You're still in your jacket! How could you have been rolling up your sleeves?'

I was so thankful for the silly banter.

Fumi-mama almost always goes for after time with a customer, but that day she invited me to her home, her gorgeous apartment in Tsukudajima. She ran a bath for me and said, 'Take your time.'

I remember seeing the night view from her bath.

When I got out of the bath, Fumi-mama said, 'OK, let's eat,' and made *chazuke*. There was plenty of rice doused with roasted green tea, plus rice bran pickles, salted seaweed and a big pickled plum. It really hit the spot, for both my body and soul.

I glanced over at Fumi-mama sitting across the table and saw that a single tear had run down her cheek. 'I'm sorry I couldn't protect you. Why did I let that guy in in the first place? It's all my fault, I'm so sorry . . .' she said, bowing her head. I jumped out of my seat and embraced her. For a little while we just hugged like that, crying.

Organiser

When I raised my head from where I'd been pressing it against Fumi-mama's chest, I saw that her sweatshirt read, 'Don't worry!' in English.

'What the heck? Fumi-mama, your loungewear is so lame.' I burst out laughing in spite of myself.

'Oh, but it's not like anyone sees it, so it's fine, isn't it?'

'Really? But you're such a perfectionist at the club.'

Ever since then I've been buying Fumi-mama fancy pyjamas and sweats for her birthday. I want her to be her lovely self every moment of every day.

So that happened, and other things happened, and I felt like I really wanted to be a strength to Fumi-mama, to make the club even more successful than it already was, so I worked hard in my own way. I was young, so companion commutes and after time didn't bother me one bit. For five years, I focused solely on work.

And my efforts paid off. I became a somewhat well-known hostess in Ginza. There's lots of scouting that happens in this business, and for a few years now I've been getting offers to work as a hired mama. But none of the contract terms or clubs themselves made me feel like it'd be worth quitting Club Fumi to take the job. Above all, I thought it was my destiny to work with Fumi-mama forever.

Then about six months ago, I got invited to go in on a project from the concept stage. The terms were so good, I was suspicious at first. But after poking around through various contacts I learned that the person who had approached me was a businessman who runs a number of food and drink establishments in Ginza and Shimbashi.

Letters from the Ginza Shihodo Stationery Shop

After mulling it over, I went to meet him about a month ago at his office in Shimbashi. He had gone independent at age twenty-five starting with a little cafe, and from there he kept opening more and more places of different types – restaurants, bars, izakaya; he was running over fifty establishments around Shimbashi, Ginza, Nihonbashi and Yaesu. And then, he told me that soon he plans to go public with his company, and to coincide with the listing, he wants to buy an entire building in Ginza, produce bars, restaurants and so on with different concepts on each floor, and open them all at once.

The ground floor will be a confectionery incorporating Japanese ingredients such as *matcha*, *azuki* and *wasanbon*. The first floor will be a cafe serving genuine English tea. The second and third floors will be a *teppanyaki* restaurant using *wagyu* and seafood caught in Japanese waters. The fourth floor will be sushi. He said the sushi will be the same restaurant as the teppanyaki, with the idea being that you can munch sushi between teppanyaki dishes or make nigiri with strips of seared wagyu. The fifth and sixth floors will be the club.

After giving me the explanation at his office, he took me over to see the building he was remodelling. The construction, including earthquake-proofing, was serious business, and the steel frame, rebar, concrete walls and so on were all exposed. The location and size were ideal, and I had the feeling that even if I were a bit demanding, everything would work out, and I'd be able to make something really great.

It was such a dream deal that I grew anxious. On the way back to the office from the construction site, I couldn't help but ask, 'Why me?'

'I heard from a number of people who regularly go to Club

Organiser

Fumi that Fumi-mama trusts you completely. Club Fumi is one of the most famous spots in Ginza, and its owner recognises your talent. That's the biggest reason.'

'Fumi-mama...'

We continued the discussion in the back seat of a domestic car that felt a little too plain for such a prosperous business person about to publicly list his company.

'In any case, there's no one else I'd consider for the position. Let's do this together.'

When he held out his hand with an earnest look in his eyes, I couldn't help but take it.

'I see... So that's how it happened.' Ken-san was thinking with a hand on his chin.

'Yes. I'm just not sure what to say to Fumi-mama... So I figured I'd write her a letter.'

'Hmm, I realise it's hard to bring up, but... I can't really recommend suddenly broaching the topic of leaving through a letter.'

'I know. I know... I tried to say it a few times. But when I see her face, I can't bring myself to.'

'Even so, I think this topic should be raised in person. The more of your story I hear, the more I feel compelled to say that.' After Ken-san spoke he began gathering the utensils on the table and putting them on the tray. 'Anyhow, perhaps you should reconsider? Please think about how Fumi-mama will feel when she suddenly receives a resignation request – and from you, whom she's cared for all these years. It's precisely the difficult messages that should be said to a person's face,' he declared, and I couldn't argue. His face had seemed so kind, but now his expression seemed spiteful. 'The reason I think it's a bad idea is that it might feel like a sneak attack. And she keeps such a watchful eye on her employees – she might have already realised. Except that since it's you, whom she's cared for all these years, she might accuse herself of over-analysing. To hand her a request for resignation if she's in that state would be too cruel.'

I heaved a sigh in spite of myself and looked up at the ceiling.

After straightening up, I stood and bowed to Ken-san.

'I realise I've been incredibly selfish and already had you bend over backwards for me, but I'm still going to ask. Please teach me how to write a resignation request that you have to give to someone you're deeply indebted to. I'll see how she's doing before I give it to her. I won't do anything cowardly like leaving it on her desk or having the general manager pass it to her. So . . . so, I'm begging you. My determination won't waver. I just want to have it as a kind of protective charm.'

I thought Ken-san might jump to his feet, but he remained seated in silence. After a little while, he spoke softly. 'Please sit down. You've already decided to leave Club Fumi and make a new start either way, right?'

'. . . Yes.'

'Then a phone call would be fine, so I think you should just tell her right now.'

How stubborn can you be? That was my honest thought. I didn't mean for it to, but my tone grew harsher.

'I can't really explain it, but it's different from quitting a normal company . . . So, so . . . please just understand.'

Ken-san closed his eyes, crossed his arms, and thought for a few moments. Then he abruptly opened his eyes and said simply, 'I guess I have no choice.' He stood up before continuing. 'It

Organiser

goes against my inclinations, but I've come this far. I'll help you. Please wait a moment while I gather the things we'll need.'

With that, he put my tea bowl on the tray and carried it away. I let out a short sigh. Looking at the clock, I saw that over an hour had passed.

Ken-san was back in less than three minutes. He brought with him paper and an envelope in plain white.

'Over here, please.'

He invited me to the large desk near the window. I picked up my Filofax, Cross pen and tote bag and approached. Ken-san put the stationery on the desk and pulled the chair out, urging me to sit.

'I think it's best to use basic stationery for a resignation request. Earlier you said "a resignation request that you have to give to someone you're deeply indebted to", but I don't think there's anyone in the world who can teach you how to write one of those. There's no way but to agonise over it until you've strung your thoughts together. Even if it comes out a bit strange, or you wrote something incorrectly, they're characters you gave your all to inscribe, so I'm sure your message will come through. And in your case, it's Fumi-mama on the receiving end, so . . .'

'. . . But if I could do that, I would have just bought some stationery at any shop and written it already.'

'Then I suppose all you can do is submit a generic request and plan on discussing it at a later time. A standard resignation request isn't very long, and if you don't make any mistakes on the envelope, you'll only need one. I'd hate to make you buy it just for that, so if you don't mind using some of my personal stock, please take this. And then . . .'

Having said that much, he took a book out of the desk

drawer, flipped to a certain page, and set it down open next to the stationery.

'You can follow the example on this page. I think the pen you brought with you will do fine.'

'Th-thank you.'

After all his reluctance, it felt a bit strange to be suddenly getting on with it.

But before my eyes was blank white paper and an envelope. All I had to do now was write it out according to the example, but my hands wouldn't move.

'You've already done so much for me, but I really don't feel like I'll be able to do a good job writing it. I don't suppose I could ask you to . . . ?'

Ken-san replied with a small shake of his head. 'There's no good or bad job when it comes to form letters like these. As long as you write carefully, you'll be fine. Read the example closely and take your time.'

'. . . OK.'

I felt like a failing student forced to take remedial after-school lessons.

'I'm sure it would be hard to write with someone watching, so I'm going to do some shopping. I'll be back in about an hour, so please hold down the fort.'

'What?'

'You don't need to answer the phone or receive deliveries. Oh, and the bathroom is over there. See you.'

With those final comments, he left.

Suddenly, I was all alone. On the desk, the paper and envelope, my Cross pen and my Filofax organiser.

Organiser

Glancing out of the window, I saw the shimmering summer air. 'Oh, a cumulonimbus.' I shifted my gaze to find the sky between the buildings blue and a pure white cloud stretching fluffily upwards. How long had it been since I'd seen such a splendid cumulonimbus?

The utterance I'd let slip to myself bumped up against the empty first floor's ceiling and was whisked away by the fan.

Right, the last time I'd seen such a big cumulonimbus was the previous year's Obon holiday. Most of our customers took holiday during that time, so Club Fumi closed up shop as well. Fumi-mama would take the opportunity to invite the hostesses and single male staff members on an overnight trip. We generally went somewhere near in the mountains or near the sea in the Kanto region, and that year we were on a beach in Chiba.

Though the party was made up of hostesses who didn't want to ruin their fair skin with a tan, Fumi-mama refused to entertain such concerns and declared, 'We're going to have a watermelon-splitting contest!' In the end, staffers went to buy a giant watermelon, and they even found a wooden sword at a souvenir shop. We spread a tarp by the hotel's pool and did the whole thing.

Even though it had been her idea, Fumi-mama came out fully equipped in long sleeves and pants, a giant straw hat and sunglasses, plus a mask and gloves, saying, 'I don't want to get sunburned either.' Everyone laughed at her – 'You look so shady!' The whole trip, Fumi-mama seemed so happy. Everyone did. And of course, I was happy too.

I opened my Filofax organiser to a pocket insert where I kept photos. A photo of everyone at our holiday dinner with Fumi-mama in the centre. Fumi-mama looking delighted to be petting a dolphin at an aquarium. A snap of the two of us standing in front of a flower arrangement that had arrived to congratulate the club on its anniversary. Tears drip-dropped onto the pocket.

In the end, I just stared blankly at the sky without writing a word. When I looked at the clock, another hour had gone by. I felt like I'd leaped forward in time, the gap between my sense and the speed of the clock was so huge.

Suddenly a voice called, 'I'm back!' from the bottom of the stairs. I hurriedly grabbed my Cross pen and pretended to be confronting the stationery.

Before long, I heard footsteps coming up. But there were two sets.

'Yuri-chan.'

I couldn't help but stand up and turn around. It was Fumi-mama standing there. And Ken-san next to her looking awkward.

'. . . Why? Why? What are you doing here?' As I spoke, the tears that had just dried overflowed again. I reflexively pressed the back of my hand against my eyes, but of course, that didn't stop them.

'The manager called me and I came rushing over. Apparently he got in touch with every customer he had who he thought might go to the club, asking if they knew how to get hold of me. We really put him out . . .'

I scowled at Ken-san. He said nothing and bowed his head.

'Yuri-chan, I'm sorry I didn't say anything, but I know that the president of Yamato Enterprise made you an offer.'

Fumi-mama approached and had me sit down. Ken-san brought one of the worktable chairs over for her.

'It must have been about a month before he spoke to you –

Organiser

Ichiki-san came to see me. Oh, during the day at my office, of course. He got straight to the point: "Would you be willing to let me have Yuri-san?" Awfully direct, but I knew instinctively from the moment we met that he was someone who could be trusted. And I knew of Yamato by reputation.'

I was utterly speechless, and what else could I be? Neither Ichiki-san nor Fumi-mama had breathed a word of this to me.

'But I'm a bit of a business person myself, you know. I couldn't let a competitor poach one of my precious employees so easily. So what I told him was, "All my hostesses and staff work of their own volition. So if she says she wants to quit, there's no way I can stop her. You ask me if you can "have" her, but Yuri isn't a possession." Ichiki-san got up from the sofa with a sober look on his face and bowed – "You're quite right. I beg your pardon." It's surprisingly rare for people to be capable of honestly admitting that they've made a mistake, so I fell even more in love with him. And after that he went to approach you directly.'

I suddenly realised Ken-san had been missing for a while.

'But why haven't you talked to me yet? I've been waiting, thinking every day, "This is the day she'll ask me about it", but nothing! Meanwhile your complexion gets more and more sickly... Did you think I would oppose it? Silly thing, this once-in-a-lifetime chance for you? Now c'mon, let me hear all the details. Is there anything I can help with?'

I had no words. I covered my face with a handkerchief I took out of my bag and continued to cry.

'Goodness, if you cry that much, your eyes are going to end up all puffy! Are you planning on calling in to work today?'

It was all I could do to nod.

*

Letters from the Ginza Shihodo Stationery Shop

We must have talked for about an hour or so? When Fumi-mama and I went downstairs, Ken-san was rearranging the postcard display.

'All done?'

'Yes, we'll get into the nitty-gritty later, but we've decided Yuri-chan will graduate from my club. I appreciate your assistance. Thank you so much for contacting me. I'll never forget it. Please come by the club sometime.'

With that, Fumi-mama bowed deeply. Ken-san returned the bow in silence.

'While I'd like to get angry and say, "How could you do such a thing?!" . . . thank you. I'm sorry I wasn't able to contribute to your sales despite ruining your day off. Once the details of my club are decided, I'll come by again to consult with you, so thank you in advance.'

'I apologise for taking things into my own hands. Please forgive me.' Ken-san straightened up before bowing. The gesture was beautiful and exuded Ginza elegance.

* * *

From Shihodo Stationery's service door came the manager, Ken Takarada. It was Wednesday, so the shop was closed as usual, and he wore chinos with a hooded sweatshirt and a field jacket over the top. It was 9:30 a.m. – late for Ken, who was the early to bed, early to rise type.

Though he usually moved with the grace of a Noh performer on stage, this morning he had the gait of a tin soldier with a broken spring. And while the cafe Hohozue was a mere five minutes from Shihodo, to look at him you would think it was a dozen kilometres, and the door as heavy as

Organiser

a castle gate. On his unsteady legs, he just made it to his usual seat.

The daughter of the cafe's owner and friend of Ken's since childhood, Ryoko, immediately brought over a hand towel and a glass of water. Ken chugged the water and pressed the cool, moist towel to his face.

'You've got the face of a drowning victim.'

'... The way you talk, it sounds like you've seen your share of drowning victims.'

'Obviously not. I'm just saying, you look that awful,' she replied coolly. 'You want a morning set?'

'Mm, just toast. The thin-sliced British-style, toasted crunchy. And to drink, milky tea. Also, I'd like to refill this water cup about a zillion times, so could you just leave a pitcher?'

'Sure,' Ryoko replied brusquely before going back to the counter.

The owner approached with the pitcher just as she left.

'How was your first visit to a club?'

'What can I even say? At the first stop, Club Yamato, I'm not even sure how many drinks I had. We toasted with champagne, then there was red wine and brandy – they treated me to all kinds of things. Then someone came to escort me to Club Fumi and I went there. The next thing I knew I was collapsed in bed. I have no idea how I got back. I guess humans must have homing instincts, too.'

'I'm jealous. Wish you would have invited me.'

Ken drank half of the fresh glass of water the owner had poured for him and heaved a big sigh.

'They wouldn't let me pay at either place. I wonder how much the bill was.'

Letters from the Ginza Shihodo Stationery Shop

The owner shook his head. 'There's no class in wondering. If you want to know, you'll just have to go again. Ah, but definitely keep it a secret from Ryoko. The first customer of the day went and blabbed, "Last night I spotted Ken-chan in 7-chome with a silly grin on his face, surrounded by pretty ladies. It was such a surprise. Has our strait-laced Ken-chan started frequenting the clubs?" so Ryoko's been in a mood all morning.'

'Hm? Why would Ryoko be in a mood?'

The owner chuckled at him and shook his head before returning to the counter.

Ken emitted a little sigh and opened the newspaper he'd unconsciously picked up from the rack by the door. But none of the words were registering, and his eyes wandered out of the window. At the other end of his absentminded gaze were people hurrying past. A scattering of them had coats on, and there were brightly coloured scarfs as well.

On a clear day during the transition between autumn and winter, the CLOSED TODAY sign was up at a little stationery shop in one corner of Ginza, and the sales floor was enveloped in silence.

Notebooks

The teapot that had contained two full cups of tea was now completely empty.

Perhaps because it was a Tuesday afternoon, the Ginza cafe Hohozue was quiet. When I looked out of the window from a two-person table, everyone I saw passing by seemed busy – I was the only one just spacing out.

This cafe, Hohozue, is where my parents used to meet up for their dates when they were young, and the owner's family is basically like part of ours. That was one reason that we stopped by whenever we came to Ginza. But that only lasted through my time in elementary school; when I actually thought about it, I realised I hadn't been in six years.

Even so, Ryoko-chan remembered me. 'Nanami-chan? Right? But wow, I was stunned for a second. You look just like Rumi when she was a high schooler. Don't come in here in a sailor uniform like that! But wait, that *is* your uniform, right, Nanami-chan?'

Yes, I was at the same school my mum and dad had graduated from. *Right, right, Ryoko-chan went there too.* That's why she was gazing at it with so much nostalgia.

'Those plain sailor outfits really take me back. So my alma mater hasn't changed the uniform in all these years. They were already rare when I was a student, so these days they're probably treated like some sort of heritage artefact, huh? Decades of the

Letters from the Ginza Shihodo Stationery Shop

exact same design. Are the boys still in those stiff collars? Wow, they haven't changed, huh? I'm kinda glad.'

We'd had that conversation an hour ago. The late lunch crowd was streaming through – I was the only one relaxing over tea – so the people in the seats around me kept changing as orders of all the popular menu items – *Naporitan* pasta, curry rice, sandwiches, hot dogs – kept coming in, and Ryoko-chan was hard at work.

Savouring my milk tea, I looked at each of the ten notebooks I'd taken out of my bag in turn and sighed. Before I knew it, it had been two hours, and I felt like I had better be going.

'Here you go – on the house. We'll be slow till evening, so you don't have to rush,' said Ryoko-chan, placing a big cup in front of me. 'It's a special sweet cafe au lait. Your mum and dad used to love it.'

Ryoko-chan's outfit featured a white blouse with a black bow tie and vest, a skirt with a tight silhouette, and low-heeled pumps. Though she had short hair and wore only light makeup, her features were such that a glance was enough for anyone to deem her beautiful. Mum said, 'Ryoko was the prettiest girl in school. When the school festival came around, droves of boys from other schools would show up – it was crazy.'

'Oh, thank you.' I hopped up and bowed to her.

'Ahh, stop, stop. It can't be good luck for me to make a customer feel that way!' she said with a smile. Then she put the empty cup and teapot on a tray and sat down across from me.

'Hey, so what're you looking at that has you sighing so much?' Her gaze fell on the notebooks I had spread across the table.

'Oh, they're club notebooks. That said, I'm retired now, so I don't need them anymore . . .'

'Handwritten notes? For a club? I thought high schoolers

Notebooks

these days all used apps for no-fuss note-taking, so that's a bit of a surprise. What club were you in?'

'Kyudo.'

'Oh, the way of the bow, huh? I see. Err, I dunno what "I see" exactly, but I feel like that somehow ties into taking handwritten notes. You said you're retired now, but it's only June. Feels a bit early.'

'Yeah, the other day we lost at a meet and as a result, we won't be advancing to the inter-high championship tournament, so I'm done.'

Ryoko-chan said, 'Aw, that's too bad.' And then, 'Oh, the kyudo club used to practise every day after school. Is that still the case? Ah, as I thought, then! Still the same. So you decided to stop by since you have extra time now that kyudo is over?'

'Well, something like that.'

Each club had its own practice schedule, with most of them meeting three times a week, but kyudo was one of the few that practised every day. Before retiring, I'd been jealous of friends in clubs with rest days who got to stop in Harajuku or Shibuya on their way home.

But now that I had free time, I didn't feel like going, even though all I had to do the next morning was attend my classes. Finally, I deviated from my route home and decided to wander Ginza between transfers. As I was walking, I suddenly recalled Hohozue and ended up here.

'How many notebooks are there?'

'Ten. About one a month.'

'Hmm. That must have been a lot of work, handwritten and all. Was it just you keeping them, Nanami-chan?'

'No, me and the captain took turns.'

Letters from the Ginza Shihodo Stationery Shop

Ryoko-chan seemed to brim with curiosity. She was super inquisitive, but it wasn't annoying; it felt like talking to an older relative.

'I was the vice-captain. In the past, it was apparently tradition to have a boy be the captain and a girl be vice-captain, but a few years ago they started deciding based on ability. The captain I was paired with did happen to be a boy, though. The previous duo were both girls. Before that, the captain was a girl and the vice-captain was a boy.'

'Oh, gender-free style, huh? Times sure have changed.'

We had gotten that far when a customer walked in.

'Irasshaimase! Really, though, take your time.' With that, she stood up and cleared the tray. From the cup rose warm steam and the sweet, gentle scents of coffee, milk and sugar.

I blew on it and took a sip. It was sweeter than I expected and tasted more like milk than coffee. Just then, I'm not sure why, but a certain flavour came to mind: the flavour of the canned coffee I drank with Takumi sitting on a bench by the bakery outside the school gate after practice – the canned coffee I was often forced to treat him to after losing our Rock, Paper, Scissors bet.

Before I knew it, tears were spilling down my cheeks and dripping onto the notebook covers. I hurriedly used a handkerchief to wipe them away and then pressed it to my eyes. But maybe that wasn't the thing to do. I couldn't stop sobbing.

I wonder how many minutes passed. Ryoko-chan came by the table with a pitcher of water.

'Feeling better?'

'. . . Sorry. I didn't mean to make a scene.'

Ryoko-chan shook her head and sat down across from me.

Notebooks

'No worries. It's slow around this time and everyone here's a regular. They're all nice grandmas and grandpas who won't be bothered. But what's the matter?'

I fell silent, unsure what to say.

'Ohhh, is this – what's it called – déjà vu? A long time ago I remember your mum crying in here after school. Does your family just have the gene for showing up here in a sailor uniform and crying?'

Her astonished tone was so silly I couldn't help but burst out laughing.

'So what is it? It must have to do with the notebooks, right? I'm pretty dense when it comes to my own business, but I'm sharp when it comes to other people's romance. All right, let's hear it.'

I replied with a little nod. 'The captain's name is Takumi Morikawa.'

'Takumi-kun, huh? What kanji does he write it with?'

'It's the character for "opening" in a pioneering way, with the hand radical on the left. And then "ocean".'

'Huh, so he's a seafarer and you're the "seven seas"? You seem like a perfect couple, at least as far as names go.'

I shook my head hard. 'We're not, though! Takumi's super popular! Nothing like me – I'm so boring.'

'Hmm, now I'm curious. Got any pictures?'

I took my phone out of my bag and showed her a few shots from the club's summer retreat.

'Ohh, he's a cutie. It's no surprise he's popular. And he looks so dashing in his *kyudogi*. I'm relieved to see he doesn't seem like a player. Of course, I haven't mastered the art of telling a person's personality from a photo alone, so I can't really say much, but looks-wise he passes, I think!'

Letters from the Ginza Shihodo Stationery Shop

Actually, I had photos of him from kyudo meets that made him look a lot cooler, but I got a bit embarrassed, so I decided not to show her.

'So you and this Takumi-kun were keeping these notebooks together. I'm getting very strong Showa vibes.'

'... Well, yes. Some students from a pretty long time ago had been keeping similar notebooks, and a couple of them were left in the *dojo*. By the time we arrived, there had been special software and apps for years, so our club was using those.'

'Well, these are the times we live in. They even give tablets and laptops to elementary schoolers these days.'

Ryoko-chan nodded at each important beat in the conversation and occasionally chimed in. It made me feel so comfortable that the words just kept flowing out of my mouth.

'Of course, for things that should be recorded as data we used apps – the number of target hits or our competition results, stuff like that. And we used our phones to record our *shakei* so we could analyse our quirks ... Oh, sorry, shakei is your shooting form.'

Ryoko-chan interjected with an 'Ohh' and with her eyes urged me to continue.

'Last June the third-years retired, and in July we took over the running of the club. At first we were imitating what the previous year's leadership had done, but Takumi and I were concerned because we had quite a lot of members who weren't improving.'

'But I'm pretty sure the kyudo faculty supervisor was ...'

'Previously, there was an advisor who had competed at nationals, but that teacher reached retirement age a few years before we arrived. The past few years a maths teacher has been

Notebooks

"advising" the club, but in name only – we can't get any coaching. The whole thing is really managed by the students.'

'Ahh, that's tough. Sounds like a lot of responsibility for the captain and vice-captain.'

It *was* really tough – I hardly remember anything about the first month after taking over the club because I was going out of my mind. In August, things finally started to settle down, but we were doing horribly in all our practice meets. Then one day, Takumi stopped me after practice.

'Still got time before curfew?'

The days had grown long, so it was still light that evening when we sent the other club members home and sat on the bench by the bakery outside the school gate.

Takumi bought canned coffee from a vending machine without a word and offered me one.

'Today's my treat. Next time we can play Rock, Paper, Scissors, and the loser can pay.'

With that unilateral declaration, he drank his coffee with audible gulps. I pulled the tab on mine and took a sip. I remember shuddering, it was so sugary.

'So the other day I was cleaning the dojo's storeroom and found some notebooks club members were keeping over thirty years ago. This is one of them.'

Takumi handed me a notebook. Someone had written in marker on the cover the name of the school, '*Kyudo Club Practice Notes*' and the names of the captain and vice-captain.

It was a Kokuyo Campus notebook, size B5 with a blue cover. The logo was placed differently from the ones I knew, but maybe that was because it was from so long ago.

Letters from the Ginza Shihodo Stationery Shop

'Take a look at this. They figured out each member's bad habits and came up with practice strategies to correct them. Awesome, right? Reading this really made me think. Like, wow, they were really serious about observing each and every member.'

Takumi sat right next to me and flipped the pages, saying, 'This, too! They took pictures of good and bad grips so they could coach the players the minute they noticed anything was off. So cool' or, 'Starting a week before a meet, they banned people from standing in front of the targets before practice officially started. Creating a simulation of the competition situation like that is an idea our generation should definitely adopt. Honestly, I have no idea why these great methods didn't get passed down . . .' – stuff like that. In any case, an hour passed in the blink of an eye.

By that point, my curfew was on my mind, so I said, 'So you're saying you want to do things like they did, right, Morikawa-kun?'

'Yeah, exactly. For starters, I bought a notebook!'

He took a brand-new Campus notebook out of his bag. It was even the same blue. He had already written the school name and '*Kyudo Club Practice Notes 1*' on it.

'Since it was my idea, I'll write my name first!'

He wrote '*Captain: Takumi Morikawa*' on the cover and handed the marker to me with the cap off.

'You gotta write your name, too, Sawamura.'

As I took the marker, I asked, 'If you're going to take the notes, why does my name need to be on it?'

'What are you talking about? You're my vice-captain, aren't you? I need your help on this.'

Succumbing to the intensity of his gaze, I wrote '*Vice-Captain: Nanami Sawamura.*'

Notebooks

'Aw man, you could've written it a little bigger . . . Well, I guess it's fine. Plus we'll probably have used this up in a month anyhow. Next time!'

Takumi tucked the notebook carefully into his bag and stood up from the bench. 'OK, guess we should head home.'

That was how it started.

'Hmm, Takumi-kun's a go-getter. So, Nanami-chan, just to confirm even though it's awkward, you haven't told him you like him yet?' Ryoko-chan asked abruptly after I told her how we started keeping the notes.

'Huh?'

This is what it means to be speechless, I thought.

'That's very Rumi of you, too.'

I just nodded without saying anything. Ryoko-chan sighed dramatically and hung her head.

'It's an honour to listen to the romance troubles of two generations – mother and daughter – and all, but couldn't you have evolved a bit? Or is DNA just that strong? Oh, I guess I was saying something similar earlier, too, huh? I heard that once you start repeating yourself it means you've officially joined the old people's club! Nooo, nooo.' Then she cracked up. I couldn't help but laugh along.

'Why don't you just say it? I don't know much about the love lives of high schoolers, but . . . you've had plenty of chances, no?'

I softly shook my head.

I'd liked him for three years, but there hadn't been any chances to tell him. No, there had been – I just didn't have the courage to say it.

*

Letters from the Ginza Shihodo Stationery Shop

During the first term of my last year of junior high, I went with my mum to an open house at the high school my parents graduated from. That was when I met Takumi.

My mum was bizarrely excited to be visiting her old school after so long, and when the welcome introduction ended, she unilaterally declared, 'You can check out clubs on your own, right? LINE me when you're done,' and went off to pay her respects to her old teachers.

That was that, so I followed the handout I'd been given at the meeting to tour the school buildings and see the gym, the music room and so on. Then I casually stopped by the *kyudojo* occupying one corner of the school grounds. At the entrance, a first-year enthusiastically invited me in – 'If you're interested, please come take a look!' – and I let the voice guide me. Just inside, there was a reception book, and after scribbling my name and school in it, an older kid led me to the seating area behind the shooting positions. Far opposite the wide-open doors, I could see little targets, and five older kids were lined up drawing their bows. At that exact moment, one of them loosed an arrow from their fully drawn bow with a beautiful sound. I found out later that the sound of the string when the arrow is loosed is called the *tsurune*. It's even the name of a popular anime. I ended up being charmed by that sound and the dignified tension of the dojo atmosphere.

'Phewww.' Someone next to me sighed. When I turned to look, I saw a boy with his eyes fixed intensely on the shooting positions. Apparently he'd been watching with bated breath. His face was suntanned, and that combined with his short hair made him seem more like the baseball or football type. It's embarrassing to admit, but it was love at first sight . . .

Notebooks

My original plan had been to watch for five or ten minutes and then leave, but since the boy remained motionless, I couldn't move. Or rather, I didn't want to. Luckily, maybe since the dojo was at the edge of the school field, there weren't any other kids observing, so he and I had the place to ourselves.

We must have been sitting there for half an hour when he abruptly spoke to me: '. . . I've made up my mind. I'm going to go to this school and join the kyudo club. What about you?'

'Huh? Ummm, I don't know. I don't even know if I'll get in or not.'

Thinking back on it now, maybe he wasn't really looking for an answer.

'Not *if* I get in: *when*. I'll pass the test. I'm getting into this school and joining the kyudo club.'

They sounded like the overly confident, grown-up words of a real piece of work, but they came off as strangely cool.

'OK, I'm gonna head out. See you when the new school year starts,' he announced, standing up without waiting for my reply, and with a silent bow towards the high schoolers, he exited the dojo.

Having been left there alone, I felt like I missed my chance to go and stayed where I was sitting for another fifteen minutes. When another kid came in with a parent, I felt like I could finally leave.

On my way out, I stopped by the reception book and saw that above my scribbled name was the name *Takumi Morikawa*. His handwriting was so neat, mature and pretty that I couldn't believe it belonged to a boy the same age as me.

And that was how Takumi Morikawa pierced my heart.

*

Letters from the Ginza Shihodo Stationery Shop

Surprising even myself, I studied hard with the goal of getting into the same high school as Takumi and joining the kyudo club. And I passed the test.

Thinking back on it now, there was zero guarantee that he would really get in as he said he would, but my belief never wavered for a moment. And Takumi did earn a place as declared.

After the entrance ceremony, I had the feeling Takumi would be waiting, so I headed to the dojo. He was there watching the older kids practise from the window. That year, spring came late, so there were still cherry blossoms where usually they would have all fallen by then.

I don't know how I can describe the way my heart leaped when I spotted Takumi's back beyond the fluttering blossoms.

When I quietly approached, he turned around.

'Hello,' I said and he nodded silently. Then he looked me straight in the eyes.

'How many months has it been? Since the open house, right?'

'. . . You remember?'

He gave me a little nod. 'Yeah. I mean, you're the only person I met here that day. I think your name was Nanami, right? Written like "seven oceans"? I checked the reception book on my way out. I'm Takumi, so I was like huh, we both have the "ocean" kanji pronounced "mi" in our name.'

'. . . Oh, huh,' I responded in an offhand way despite the swell of happiness inside me. *Takumi remembered my name!*

'Yeah, so what are you going to do? I'm going to join the club as I said back then. Though I don't want to stick out in a weird way, so I'll wait until the trial period starts. You?'

'I guess I'm still thinking.'

You idiot! Why can't you just be honest and say, 'You said you were going to get into this school and join the kyudo club – that's why I got in here and I'm going to join the club, too'?!

'Oh. Well, there are a lot of different clubs. Having a hard time making up your mind is normal.'

'. . . Yeah.'

That was how I missed my first chance to tell him. And from then until we became captain and vice-captain, there were any number of chances, but I wasted them all.

'Hey Takumi, another girl from my class said she wants your LINE.'

It was just after the meeting of second-years during our summer retreat ended. Everyone was getting ready to go and one of the boys said that to Takumi.

'And?' he answered flatly.

'Don't worry, I didn't give it to her! I went ahead and leaked how cold and boring your messages are. And I made sure to let her know I'm far more interesting and quicker at replying.'

'OK, that's fine then.'

'Ah, you never change, do you? You don't even wonder who it was?'

Takumi shook his head. 'Nope. Or more like, it doesn't matter if I wonder or not. I decided I won't be dating anyone while I'm captain of the kyudo team. Even assuming we make it to the inter-high championship tournament, we only have a little over a year left. I want to put all my time into the club. So even if I were "going out" with someone, I wouldn't be able to go on any dates, and I don't think I could do long phone calls or LINE chats. That would be pretty rude, right?'

Letters from the Ginza Shihodo Stationery Shop

Hearing him say that gave me super mixed feelings. I didn't have to worry about anyone stealing him away from me, but in exchange for that peace of mind, there would be no chance of me getting together with him either. I deeply regretted not telling him how I felt back during our first year.

And on the flip side of that regret were justifications to protect myself: *I'm not a match for Takumi. I'm sure he only thinks of me as a fellow kyudo club member. It's way better to say nothing than confess my feelings and make things awkward . . .* My mind meandered back and forth like that.

'Hmm, Takumi-kun's hardcore. I was under the assumption that high schoolers these days were more casual about dating, so that's a surprise.'

'It depends on the person. There are other people in the kyudo club who are dating.'

When I glanced to the side I saw the owner sigh with a scowl and shake his head.

'Sorry to interrupt, Nanami-chan. Ryoko, you completely forgot Ken-chan's delivery, didn't you? You're gonna starve the poor guy to death!' he said, handing Ryoko-chan a thermos and a basket.

'Oh no, I totally forgot . . . Drat!'

She stood up in a rush and grabbed my hand.

'Hey, you should come with me. There's this stationery store, Shihodo, right nearby. I need to deliver something to the manager. If I go alone, he'll pick on me forever about being late. C'mon, please?'

'Ken-chan's not like that,' the owner sighed with an eye roll. 'Oh, that's right. Nanami-chan, he's another graduate of your

Notebooks

school. Same class as your mum, dad and Ryoko. I'm sure he'll be surprised to see you, so go say hi. In exchange your bill can be *roha*,' he said.

'Roha?' I repeated in spite of myself. Ryoko told me it was old slang for 'free' because of the way the parts of the kanji character look like katakana characters that say 'roha'.

'Now hurry up!' Ryoko-chan set the thermos and basket on the counter for a minute to pull a navy cardigan off a shelf and put it on. I rushed to pack my notebooks and phone into my bag and followed Ryoko-chan out of Hohozue.

'Take care. Say hi to Ken-chan for me!' With the owner's voice at our backs, we hurried down the alley past its rustling willow tree branches.

After walking for about five minutes, a cylindrical postbox like you might see in an illustration appeared, and across from it was the stationery shop.

'Ken-chan, I'm so sorry!' Upon opening Shihodo's glass door, Ryoko-chan pressed her palms together. The manager 'Ken-chan' was standing just inside the door.

'. . . I'll never forgive you. As punishment, you're sentenced to watch the shop until I finish eating.' The way he teased her so playfully in this exaggerated, theatrical tone made it instantly clear how close their relationship was.

'Oh! Irasshaimase . . .'

When he spotted me hidden behind Ryoko-chan, he hurriedly uncrossed his arms and greeted me, speechless, before blurting, 'Wait! R-Rumi?!'

'Right? She looks just like her. But this is Nanami-chan, Rumi and Sawamura-kun's daughter.'

Letters from the Ginza Shihodo Stationery Shop

'Nice to meet you. I'm Nanami Sawamura. Just stopping by . . .'

When I introduced myself, he said, 'Ohh? Ahh . . . S-sorry, I haven't been this shaken in a while. My humble apologies. Ken Takarada of Shihodo, at your service,' with a low bow.

Ryoko-chan and I smiled to see him so flustered.

'Tch, what the heck. If that's what this is, you could've LINE'd me before coming over . . . But hmm, Rumi-chan's daughter, huh? Oh, please call me Ken-chan,' he said. 'Hrm, but yeah, Rumi and Sawamura did get married, didn't they?'

'Yeah,' said Ryoko-chan. 'After we graduated high school, they started living together in Sawamura-kun's apartment and had Nanami-chan almost immediately. It's pretty rare to date in high school, get married and have a kid while you're still a teenager. That's just how passionate their love was . . . In a way, I'm envious.'

'In a way? What way is that?' asked Ken-chan.

'. . . Does it matter?'

As Ryoko-chan spoke, she spread a cloth over a little table next to the checkout counter and laid out an oval, stainless steel plate and a perfectly white coffee mug. On the plate was a toasted sandwich and French fries. Then she placed a moist towel on a bamboo dish, set out a creamer of milk and a sugar bowl, and poured coffee from the thermos into the mug.

'Sorry I kept you waiting. Bon appetit!'

'Normally I would never eat in front of a customer, please excuse me,' Ken-chan apologised before scooting the folding chair closer to the table, wiping his hands with the towel, and chomping into the sandwich with an *'Itadakimasu!'*

'Agh, if you scoff it like that you'll get it on your shirt!'

'I mean, I reserved for one-thirty and you're over an hour late – I'm starving! Though even if you had delivered it on time, I was crazy busy until a little while ago, so I wouldn't have been able to eat anyhow,' Ken-chan said, sticking out his tongue. 'So, Nanami-chan, was it? What is Sawamura's daughter, the spitting image of Rumi, doing out on delivery with Ryoko-chan? Oh, not that I'm bothered – you're more than welcome. After all, high school girls use the most stationery of anyone.'

Ryoko-chan piped up in annoyance. 'I'm glad you're passionate about your business and all, but should you really be sales-talking a high schooler?'

'Nanami-chan, you see how difficult the world of adults is . . . Just kidding. Oh, but are Sawamura and Rumi doing well?'

I briefly explained how Dad had been transferred to Osaka for work and how Mum was doing admin at a medical clinic. 'Um, do you mind if I take a look around the shop?'

'Of course not! By all means, go right ahead. Please take your time.'

His tone was suddenly formal again. It was like he instantaneously flipped back into work mode.

'You don't have to buy something just to buy something!' Ryoko-chan said with a chuckle.

'Oh c'mon, was that really necessary?' muttered Ken-chan. They really got along so well. *Wish I had a relationship like that.*

There was a regular meet coming up, and Takumi and I got into our first fight over the boys' shooting order. It was November.

In the singles tournament in October, Takumi had made it to fifth, but missed out on making top three for a medal. And we entered eight teams – four girls' and four boys' – in the three-shooter *tachi* competition, but none of them got very good results, and no one made it to the next round.

'I want to have someone who won't miss their first shot as *omae*. I'm the one with the highest rate of nailing my first shot, so I'm going first,' Takumi said on our usual bench, as if it had already been decided. That day I'd lost Rock, Paper, Scissors again and was taking a sip of the canned coffee I'd bought. The season had just flipped so the machines sold it hot.

The next team competition would be teams of five, with each school limited to submitting one boys' team and one girls' team; only the seven, including two alternates, listed on the rosters were allowed to attend. Who those seven would be, all the second-years had decided together, but the meeting ended with everyone leaving the shooting order up to the captain and vice-captain.

'But who'll be the *ochi*, then?'

From first to last, the positions in a five-shooter tachi are called: *omae*, *niteki*, *naka*, *ochimae* and *ochi*. Most teams had their captain shoot last, ochi, to lead the team from the rear. But Takumi was saying he, the captain, wanted to shoot omae. Incidentally, for the girls, we had made a no-fuss decision that I would shoot ochi.

'I'll have Kihara do it.'

Kihara-kun was the only first-year who had been chosen to participate in the team competition.

'He can't shoot ochi at his first ever five-tachi!' I resisted. Eight second-years and nine first-years – a total of seventeen boys – had competed for the seven slots. The second-years talked it over, considering everyone's rate of hitting the target during the previous two weeks of regular practice sessions as well as past competition results. During the meeting, Takumi pushed hard for Kihara-kun and squeezed him onto the roster. Because of that, two of the second-years wouldn't be able to participate.

'Maybe not, but there's no point in putting him somewhere safe like niteki or ochimae. I want him to be the next captain. I want him to experience what it's like to take on an important role.'

'. . . He already has to deal with everyone being envious that he's the only first-year on the roster.'

'Kihara's not the type to let a blip like that get him down. And if it does, then he just couldn't hack it,' Takumi said coldly.

'I dunno. This isn't like you, Morikawa-kun. I don't think anyone will agree with that order,' I found myself saying before I realised it. Hearing my own voice, the way I seemed to be pushing him away startled me. When I quickly looked back at him, he was staring up at the dark sky in silence.

I fell silent too and just stared at his face in profile. From the side, his distinct features and long eyelashes stood out even more. After a little while, he let out a short sigh.

'I just really want to win . . . I know I'm making everyone work too hard. I changed up the practice drills, and even though I said morning practice is voluntary, I've gotten almost everyone to attend. So I want to win and be happy together. To that end, I want to figure out how to win, even if it means being a little unreasonable.'

I could tell he was desperate. But there were actually a handful of team members rebelling, and the role of going around calming them down fell to me.

'But . . . but look, Morikawa-kun. It might be the case that not everyone in the club feels the same way you do. I mean, I'm sure everyone wants to win. But I think there are also people who just want to enjoy kyudo or who just want to draw their bows and make friends. You should consider their feelings too.'

Takumi was gazing intently at my face. But then he shook his head without replying. 'Sorry, I'm gonna go home. Let's talk more tomorrow.'

With that, he left me sitting there. Watching his back recede, I nursed my no-longer-hot coffee. For some reason, once he turned the corner, I was crying. I set my can of coffee on the ground, pressed a handkerchief to my eyes and audibly sobbed. I regretted not being able to say, *I feel the same way as you, Takumi!*

But saying that would have been tantamount to abandoning my role as vice-captain. I'd been suppressing my own feelings ever since he'd handed me the practice notes notebook and said, 'You're my vice-captain', so . . .

Suddenly, I felt a pat on my head. When I looked up, startled, it was Takumi standing there.

'. . . Are you OK?'

No, I'm not! I thought as I nodded. 'My contact lens was slipping . . . But it's better now, so I'm fine. I thought you went home.'

'Huh? Oh, I just realised maybe it was pretty awful of me to go home first after making you stay late. C'mon, let's go. We have morning practice tomorrow, you know.'

He picked up my bag and set off walking. I hurried after him and took my bag when he offered it.

'Today it's your turn, right, Sawamura? To do the notebook. Write down the order you want the boys to go in. I'll take a look and keep thinking . . .' he said, keeping his gaze facing forward. 'I know you do a lot of coordinating for me. And I realise that when the club feels like it's going to go scattering apart, you're the one holding it together ... So I guess I'm sorry ... for being so self-centred all the time.'

I felt like I was going to cry again. I quickly pressed my handkerchief to my eyes.

'What, your contact lens again?'

'I-I'm fine!'

I could only manage to fake it enough to say that much.

Our fourth notebook was nearly full, and that night, I reread all of them front to back. As I worked out the status of each club member, from the start of the first notebook to the end of the fourth, I gradually began to understand what Takumi was getting at.

When I compared the days Takumi had taken notes to the days I had, it became obvious that we were looking at totally different things. Takumi was making detailed shakei observations.

The principles of shooting differ somewhat depending on what school of kyudo, but there are eight of them called the *shaho hassetsu*: *ashibumi* – determining your footing; *dozukuri* – nocking the arrow and adjusting your posture; *yugamae* – putting your right hand's fingers on the string; *uchiokoshi* – raising the bow overhead; *hikiwake* – drawing the bow apart with the left and right hands equally; *kai* – finishing the draw and aiming; *hanare* – opening the chest and loosing the arrow; *zanshin* – remaining in hanare posture while observing where the arrow strikes.

Takumi was observing the habits of each club member through each step of the hassetsu, even finding differences between free practice, regular practice and practice meets. An archer with a high hit rate in free practice might get nervous when records were being taken in regular practice and miss more often; or some kids were stable at our school's dojo, but couldn't

Letters from the Ginza Shihodo Stationery Shop

perform well at other venues. His notes made all these characteristics easy to understand.

My notes, on the other hand, covered both practice and break time and mainly focused on what people were talking about, tracking their feelings, and so on – I highlighted things that came up in conversation and stuck out to me. Though, I also left big sticky notes that said 'Once you read this, throw it away!' with things I didn't want to leave on record, so some critical parts had to be filled in via memory.

In the end, it was nearly dawn by the time I finally managed to come up with my shooting order.

I went to morning practice having underslept and handed Takumi the notebook. He took a glance and said, 'Me omae and Kihara niteki?' in a low voice. And then, 'Tell me why.'

'If your goal is to cultivate Kihara-kun, then I think you should position him where he can see everything you do from the closest vantage point. And then, rethinking your idea that we should have someone least likely to miss their first shot shoot omae, I agreed. And if we had you go ochi, Kihara-kun wouldn't be able to watch you closely no matter which position we put him in.'

Takumi smiled with a little nod and said, 'OK. We'll go with your proposal.'

Shihodo was a surprisingly large store with tall shelves that made it feel almost maze-like. I went around exploring with Ryoko-chan and Ken-chan's animated voices in the background.

There were rows of stationery sets, postcards, greeting cards and then a section for notebooks and memo pads.

There were brands of notebooks and memo pads I'd never

seen before along with plenty of the Kokuyo Campus series. Naturally, they had the B-ruled B5 size that Takumi and I had been using for our practice notes, but even just looking at the ruling, there were five different types – A, B, C, U and UL. Others had graph paper or vertical lines, or no lines at all. Some had dots on the lines to make it easier to write neatly.

'I had no idea there were this many kinds,' I murmured to myself before I realised it.

Takumi insisted on using the B-ruled B5 Campus notebook, stubbornly refusing any other type. Once we went to the stationery shop near school together, but he made a beeline for the usual notebook, paid immediately and walked straight out again.

'Hey, you don't want to try a different kind now and then? There are so many designs. We could pick something cuter, or cooler. They even had ones with traditional binding,' I said, but Takumi shook his head emphatically.

'I'm the type to approach things through form. If I'm copying something, I want to copy every detail. We're modelling this practice on our predecessors', and they always used B-ruled Kokuyo Campus notebooks. Unfortunately, we can't meet them to ask why they chose these specific notebooks, but I'm sure there must have been some reason. So until I master this format in my own way, I want to keep using them.'

Takumi sometimes said things that were hard to understand. Unable to come up with a reply, I nodded silently.

He said he was copying our predecessors, but the way he filled out the notebook was full of his own innovations. Every time I was in awe, like, *How many different kinds of pens can you possibly use?!*

Letters from the Ginza Shihodo Stationery Shop

He would write mainly in black and then draw blue borders around positives and wavy red lines below negatives. On top of that, he would write things he thought were important with a brush pen or marker, highlight things for emphasis, etc. Even though I was the only one who would ever read them, he put a lot of thought into the format.

I knew I couldn't compete with Takumi in terms of content, but I took cues from the pages he wrote and added visual aids. Takumi would laugh and say, 'This is too much!'

But he also, without fail, would write little comments like, 'Wow! I didn't notice that . . . Good catch!' or 'Yes, yes, exactly' or 'Not quite. Let's discuss it.' It was such a small gesture, but the thought that he was actually reading my notes made me happy.

I wanted to write thoughtful comments on his pages, too, but everything he said made so much sense to me that all I could say was, 'I agree!' or 'Got it!'

Across from the notebook section were all sorts of writing instruments. Mechanical pencils, ballpoint pens, felt-tip pens, highlighters, brush pens. They were organised by brand and series, arranged by colour and thickness in precisely partitioned containers. *How many kinds are there?* The view was so spectacular it made me wonder.

Even among the pens I knew, there were unusual ink colours like purple, brown and yellow, and they came in a whole range of thicknesses from ultra-thin to ultra-thick.

I was surprised to see that even the brush pens came in varieties adults would use like black or grey, but also all sorts of colours that you could use to draw pictures.

To high school girls who didn't participate in any clubs,

Notebooks

maybe a stationery shop like this was taken for granted to the point that it wouldn't even be worth mentioning in conversation.

Maybe Takumi had looked around a big stationery shop like this before settling on the Kokuyo Campus notebook. And for the pens, too, he may not have been playing with different colours, but maybe he made a keen search for high-quality pens.

After passing the shelves where the pens and notebooks were facing each other, a huge poster leaped into my field of vision: 'It's club retirement season! Say thank you to your *senpai* or send a message to that cute *kohai*.'

Beneath the poster was regular coloured card-stock paper as well as some in the shapes of balls from sports like basketball, volleyball and rugby; a football helmet; tennis rackets and ping pong paddles; a badminton shuttlecock, and so on. Smartly designed cut-outs, cards and autograph books were featured in the crowded display. Other designs included – I suppose for the band kids – wind instruments and musical scores, guitars and drums for the light music club, and even spotlights and stage designs for the dance and theatre kids. There were also felt-tip pens and markers of all different colours as well as stamps.

But there wasn't anything that brought to mind a bow. The only martial arts stuff I could find were an autograph book with kendo protective gear on the cover and a cut-out that must have been a uniform for karate or judo or something.

That said, our kyudo club didn't have a whole retirement ceremony or anything. The convention was simply that as soon as we were knocked out of the competitions, the third-years stopped showing up to practise and the second-years took over operations. So no one exchanged cards. If anything, the third-years handed down practice gear like quivers or straw target stands to second-years around the time of their graduation ceremony.

The exception to the lack of commemoration was the changing of the captain and vice-captain roles. We would do that this coming Saturday. Takumi had already given the key to the dojo to the next captain, Kihara-kun, but there were other things to pass on, such as the bank book and seal for the account containing our club funds and the contact list of other schools for setting up regular practice meets.

Completing those formalities would be the last job Takumi and I did together as captain and vice-captain.

Come to think of it, it was about a year ago, after Takumi and I had taken over things from the third-years, that he had said, 'Hey, do you have a second?' It was just after the third-years had left the dojo, and just the two of us remained.

'Hm?'

'So, I've been thinking . . . How about we make sure that the upperclassmen take point on the odd jobs around the dojo? I don't mean to criticise our senpai, but I want to quit letting third-years take it easy while the kohai do all the prep and cleanup.'

The sudden proposal caught me off guard.

'First-years are busy enough just getting used to practising – we know what that's like. If we make them do all the prep and cleanup on top of that, they might end up hating kyudo, don't you think? I don't want anyone to quit the club. That would be awful, right?'

It seemed out of character.

'Hey, what's that smirk for?' Takumi got genuinely mad at me.

'I'm not smirking. I'm just a bit surprised. I mean, we did prep

Notebooks

and cleanup as first-years, didn't we? And you put in so much effort, coming early to set up so you wouldn't get told off by our senpai, staying late to make sure everything was put away perfectly . . . So why change things this year?'

'I don't want to perpetuate something I think is unfair. Why should the upperclassmen steal practice time from lowerclassmen while not doing a thing? So I want to change it with my — no, our — era. What do think? Is my idea totally off base?'

I thought about it for a moment. What Takumi was saying made sense, but I wondered if the rest of the kids in our grade would agree.

'I understand how you feel, Morikawa-kun . . . So, what do the other guys our age think about it?'

'Huh?' Takumi looked surprised. 'I haven't asked anyone yet, so I don't know.'

'You gotta be kidding me! You went and decided something this important without talking to anyone?!'

'Not without talking to anyone — I'm talking to you right now, Sawamura. And I didn't decide it — like I said, it's an idea.'

I didn't know what to do. What Takumi was saying was correct, and the idea of beginning a new tradition under our leadership where everyone works together to prep and cleanup was attractive. The issue was how to get all the other members to agree . . .

'I'll talk to the guys one by one and get their approval. So I want you to get the girls onboard. If possible, I'd like to make the announcement at the meeting before practice this coming Monday. Do you think you can talk to everyone today or tomorrow?'

'. . . I'll try.'

Takumi suddenly held out his right hand. Then he took my right hand, and brought in his left hand as well to squeeze it.

'I'm counting on you. Making a good start is critical. Let's maintain the good traditions, reform anything we feel is unreasonable and make this the best kyudo club ever.'

'... OK.'

It may have just been a handshake, but with Takumi asking me with his hands squeezing mine, I couldn't say no.

That night I was so giddy I presented my passionate argument to all the second-year girls.

'It kinda sounds more like your opinion than Morikawa-kun's, Nanami-chan...'

In the end, everyone was a bit put out but accepted the proposal.

'Oh, this display is perfect for Nanami-chan!'

When I glanced to my side I saw Ryoko-chan standing there.

'Are you done with your delivery?'

'Yeah, he's a fast eater. No matter how many times I tell him to savour the flavours, he never listens.'

Ken-chan walked over to us. 'I couldn't eat it that fast if it didn't taste good. I'm actually expressing how tasty it is with my entire body, so I wish you'd just be happy.'

'You've always got some slick excuse.'

Disregarding Ryoko-chan's mild annoyance, Ken-chan said to me, 'Please let me know if there's anything you're interested in. I have samples of popular products out, but anything can be opened up for a closer look if you like.'

It seemed his late lunch had restored his energy.

'Uh, do you have anything for kyudo club?'

'Yes, one moment please. Umm . . .' After a beat, he produced a target-shaped card from the back of the display. 'This is a Shihodo original. Though it hasn't been selling as well as hoped . . . As you know, kyudo targets are usually black and white, but since it would be hard to write a message on the black part, we made it this blue-green colour. I guess people who are actually into kyudo can't help but feel like the colours are off, so the response hasn't been great. Also I guess it's hard to get the oval shape to stand up. Those seem to be some of the reasons it hasn't been popular.' Then he said, 'I did make it the same size as a regulation target – one *shaku* and two *sun*. I guess I'll have to rethink it for next year . . . Also, it'd be a special order, but I know an independent creator who can be commissioned for illustrations. It's possible to make stickers, too.'

'O-oh, that's OK. I don't actually plan to use it . . .' I hurriedly shook my head.

'Oh, I know. What about giving a card to your captain to thank him for all his hard work. And you could tell him how you feel on top of it,' Ryoko-chan whispered in my ear like a sneak attack. My face must have turned bright red. Ken-chan looked puzzled for a moment, but quickly recovered his composure.

'If there's something I can help with, don't hesitate to let me know – anything at all. I'll do everything in my power to fulfil your request.'

There was something about Ken-chan – maybe his earnest tone of voice, or stance, I guess? – but he was starting to remind me of Takumi.

The third term of our second year had just started. Once we entered the new year, the temperature had plummeted, and despite the roof, once the doors were open to the field, the dojo was freezing cold. Cold bodies tend to tense up, and in the winter, the number of club members who slip into shrunken postures increases. I'm not great with the cold, either, so even knowing all that, it still affected my performance.

One day Takumi had handed over the notebook, I saw that he had given me a bunch of detailed notes on my shooting form. The one that caught my attention the most was the comment written with big brush pen strokes: *'Your kai is too short! You're rushing!'*

'Nnngh . . .'

I was sitting in my room alone reviewing the notebook when my phone buzzed. I was surprised to find it was a message from Takumi.

'Did you see the notes?'

Maybe he's not great at typing on a phone? He always writes short messages.

'I just saw,' I wrote back just as clipped.

'Can you talk now?'

I was thinking, *Huh? What? That's kind of sudden!* but he was already calling me without even waiting for a reply.

'Er, hello? What is it?'

Ugh, couldn't I have answered in a cuter way?

'Hey, sorry it's so late. I heard rushing is a hard problem to fix, so I was worried . . .'

'Oh, yeah. Right. And I did realise . . . But like you said, it's been getting worse lately, and I've been feeling unsure what to do about it.'

'Oh, you knew? Then you need to make a conscious effort to fix it. What are you gonna do?'

Notebooks

He could ask me 'What are you gonna do?' out of the blue all he wanted, but I hadn't found any ways to fix it, so I didn't have a response. When I said nothing, he said, 'Are you listening?'

'Oh, yeah, I'm listening. Nnngh, what should I do?'

'So I was thinking in the train on the way home that a return to basics, doing some *sobiki*, might be good.'

Huh? I thought. *He was thinking about me his whole train ride home?*

'Sobiki . . . ? Like a first-year, huh?'

Sobiki is practising drawing your bow without nocking an arrow.

'Yeah, so I was thinking maybe not at school, but at home a few times before bed. Of course, you'd have to take your bow home every day . . .'

The bow is seven shaku, three sun long – that is 221 centimetres – so you have to be careful when changing trains and whatnot not to get in people's way. When we have competitions, a whole bunch of us are travelling with our bows, so part of the vice-captain's job is to make sure everyone is walking with an awareness of their surroundings.

'. . . Sobiki at home. Sounds like a pain, but you're right that it might help.' I said it as if we were talking about someone else's training schedule, irritated by my own coldness.

'Yeah, it might be kind of rough, so I'll do it with you. Let's do it together.'

'Huh? What do you mean?' Even I could tell my voice came out as a yelp.

'I wouldn't feel right making you do something annoying like that all by yourself. Plus it's a good chance for me to re-examine my shakei. How about this? We'll bring our bows home every day for a month. When it's a good time for you, you can LINE me. Then I'll get ready and do sobiki practice with you. Hmm, how about . . . thirty times? Go through each of the hassetsu one by one, making sure you take a good ten seconds for the kai. The point is to take your time and really pay attention to what you're doing, so I think thirty is plenty.'

'If you're prepared to do it then I suppose I can give it a try.'

That was how our two-person intensive training programme began.

'About to start.'

Whenever I sent that message, Takumi would reply with just 'OK.' Doing a mindful thirty draws according to his advice took between thirty and forty minutes. And when I sent, 'Finished' he would reply with a 'Nice work!' LINE sticker. It was only a brief exchange, but it made me happy.

Incidentally, in order to do a proper uchiokoshi, you need at least three and a half metres of vertical space. The only place I could do it in my house was the entryway, where the ceiling was double height. I found out later that Takumi couldn't do it inside, so he'd been drawing his bow in his yard. It was the middle of the night in the middle of winter, so he must have been freezing.

In this way, I was able to fix my rushing habit by the spring tournament in February. Then one night after reporting that I'd finished, he sent me the usual 'Nice work!' sticker and . . .

'I don't think you're rushing anymore. So this can be our last intensive training day.' He sent a 'You did it!' sticker.

That was how our two-person intensive training programme came to an abrupt end.

Notebooks

I felt like I had to say something, but I just reread our message history – the same messages every day – over and over. Before I knew it, my phone screen was wet with tears.

It was all I could do to send a sort of silly 'Thank youuuu' sticker in reply.

'Hey, are you OK?'

It was when I heard Ryoko-chan's voice that I realised I was crying again. *What's up with me today?*

'Ryoko, the first floor is open today, so why don't you have her take her time?'

Ryoko murmured an 'OK' and put a hand gently on my back to guide me to the staircase.

The first floor had big windows, and the space was enveloped in soft sunlight. At the back on the right was a raised area covered in tatami, and in the open central area, worktable-like islands were arranged in a rectangle. The entire left-hand wall from floor to ceiling was packed with drawers and sliding-door cupboards, so overall it felt like a school's art room.

I noticed a desk on the left in the back. Ryoko-chan must have seen my eyes shift towards it because she said, 'It's quite a desk, huh?'

She ushered me over and pulled out the chair for me.

'Here you go.'

The chair had a sturdy leather seat and seemed to be made of the same wood as the desk. I laid my arms on the top of the desk and ran my palms over it. The rough feel was pleasant. I thought if I just put my head down and cried I might feel better, but I couldn't very well do that in front of Ryoko-chan.

'Well, not to be rude, but I'm gonna head back to the cafe to return the dishes. If it's not crowded, I'll be right back. So just wait here for a little while, OK?'

With that, she hurried down the stairs. Maybe it had been unconscious, but the way she said, 'I'll be right back', made it sound like she felt at home at the shop.

I took the Kyudo Club Practice Notes notebooks out of my bag. For each of the ten notebooks, Takumi had neatly written, '*Kyudo Club Practice Notes*' on a cream-coloured label and stuck it on the spine. His penmanship was precise, and when you lined up the notebooks from one to ten, all the characters were in perfect alignment, not a single stroke out of place.

From the top of each notebook reached sticky notes marking pages with important info or anything Takumi felt like he needed to reread multiple times. The notes themselves were crammed full of characters recording when he'd last looked at the page. Every page had comments emphasised with different colours, thicknesses and sizes, and each comment brimmed with memories of practice sessions. As Takumi had declared in front of his peers, he had dedicated his entire year as captain to the kyudo club. These notebooks were proof of it.

I opened the tenth notebook to the last page Takumi had written on. The date was Sunday, the day our retirement was decided.

He noted the results of the girls' and boys' competitions and then left thorough comments on each club member's individual performance. It was the Tokyo Prefecture qualifiers for the inter-high tournament, so if we lost, it meant immediate retirement for the third-years. Five shooters, four shots per person, for a total of twenty shots. The top eight teams would advance. Sadly, both the boys and the girls were a point short of going through to the semi-finals. Incidentally, the individual qualifiers were at the same time and Takumi, who hit the target with all four of his shots, did get through. But maybe the team getting knocked out really shocked him? He went on to hit only two of four and didn't manage to get a medal.

Despite that, without touching on whether the results were good or bad, he wrote about whether each member had been able to apply what they'd been working on in practice during the runup to the competition or not. I'm not sure how he was able to be so composed when, as the captain, he was probably feeling the most upset of anyone.

There were notes on my shooting as well. 'Despite being busy with administrative odds and ends for the club, she was able to shoot true to form. No sign of rushing. The dignity befitting the vice-captain was evident in her calm performance.'

'Honestly, he sounds like a faculty advisor or something...' I murmured aloud in spite of myself.

At the bottom of the page, it said:

Dear Vice-Captain Nanami Sawamura,

Great work this year. I know I caused a lot of trouble for you with all my unreasonable demands. I'm sorry. And thank you. I truly have nothing but gratitude.

Unfortunately, we never managed to place in the top three and get a medal. But I think we can be proud of the fact that no one, not in our grade, or younger, quit the club.

And that's thanks to you, Sawamura. If it weren't for your being vice-captain, I think people would have run out of patience with me long ago, and probably lots of them would have quit.

That said, I feel really bad when I think that if you hadn't

Letters from the Ginza Shihodo Stationery Shop

been in this role, there were lots of other fun things you could have been doing outside the club. I'm sure there were other things you wanted to do. I'm sorry I worked you so hard.

Now we have to get ready for university entrance exams, so we can't exactly take it easy, but I hope you can enjoy the rest of your high school life.

Once again, Thank you.

Captain Takumi Morikawa

The thank-you at the end had maybe been written in brush pen – the characters were big and strong. Tears fell every time I reread his message, and some of the text had bled. And this day, too, I accidentally added some more smudges.

I had found this notebook in my shoe cubby the previous day when I arrived at school. Really, I was meant to write in it during the day yesterday and return it to Takumi, but I just couldn't get myself to do it. In the end, I borrowed the other nine notebooks from the shelf in the dojo and reread them all, but I still couldn't figure out what to say.

No, that's not true. What I wrote wasn't important. I just hated the fact that our notebook correspondence would come to an end once I replied . . . but I had no idea what to do about it.

When I glanced to my side, I saw Ken-chan had shown up with a tray.

'I made some tea. And there's a *mame daifuku* if you're in the mood for something sweet,' he said, arranging the tea bowl and daifuku plate on the desk. When I moved to stand up, he gestured with a hand to stop me, and continued speaking, his gaze falling on the notebooks.

Notebooks

'This may sound rude, but it's so quintessentially high school – Campus notebooks. Maybe especially the B5 size.'

'... Yeah. You don't really use notebooks as an adult?'

Ken-chan cocked his head slightly as he considered my question. 'I feel like people do take notes in them. But these days it's easy to do various things on your phone or tablet, so I think the number of people using notebooks has been on the decline. Of course, there's also a contingent of people who insist on notebooks, so for them there are deluxe models using fine paper, and customisable products for which you can choose the cover, page designs and even the binding are popular. Shihodo makes original products and we take custom orders, too.'

'Oh wow, huh ...'

I had no idea. Maybe Takumi would like a custom notebook as a present?

'It might be odd to say this, given we have our own line of notebooks, but the Kokuyo Campus series are highly polished products. I have to hand it to them when it comes to comparing what you get to the price. And really, notebooks are meant to be written in and used up one after the other. You have about ten of them there, right? I'm sure they're happiest when they're well-used like that.'

The gaze Ken-chan poured down on the practice notes Takumi and I kept was warm and gentle. Maybe it made sense because he ran a stationery shop, but his massive love for writing supplies came through clearly.

'... But on Sunday, we lost, so we're already retired. That means this is also the end of the practice notebooks.'

In the notebook open in front of me was the 'Thank you'

Letters from the Ginza Shihodo Stationery Shop

message from Takumi. It was big enough that Ken-chan probably saw it from where he was standing.

'Well, I'm not sure what to say, but . . . if there's a beginning, that means there will be an end. But it's precisely because there's an end that there can be a new beginning. What if you tried thinking about it like that?' Then he said, 'Anyhow, here's the tea and daifuku. I'll be back shortly,' and went down the stairs. *Ryoko-chan, Ken-chan – everyone's saying they'll be back soon and then going down those stairs.*

The thought kind of cracked me up and I couldn't help but laugh. I closed the tenth notebook, set it atop the other nine, and picked up the tea bowl. The fragrant green tea was delicious. There was a toothpick on the plate with the daifuku, but I didn't feel like bothering with it and instead I pinched the whole thing between my fingers and bit off about half of it. The mochi was just the right amount of chewiness, and the bean paste wasn't too sweet, which made for an exquisite mame daifuku – that was delicious, too.

I'd been crying so much, but a yummy snack was enough to make me feel better – *Be serious*, I thought, somewhat offended by myself.

At the sound of footsteps jogging up the stairs, I quickly wiped my mouth with my handkerchief.

'Sorry I kept you waiting. Please use this. Oh, you don't have to pay. It's a present to mark your first visit to the shop.' With that, Ken-chan handed me a brand-new Campus notebook. It was a B-ruled, B5 size notebook – the exact same kind as Takumi and I had been using for our practice notes.

'Huh? Err, um . . .'

Unsure what was going on, exactly, I got flustered, and

Notebooks

Ken-chan continued in a calming tone. 'Well, well, no need to stress. I don't know the whole situation, so I could be wrong, but I get the sense you'd like to continue your notebook correspondence with this guy?'

'But . . .'

But what? I didn't really know, myself. Ken-chan neither agreed nor disagreed, just accepted my murmur with a slight nod.

'I've only seen the cover and the page with the big characters that was open before, so I might be off base, but my sense from his neat yet free and easy handwriting is that Takumi-kun – was it? – is an upstanding, hardworking person. I'm sure he must have proposed a lot of things to proactively lead you as his vice-captain over the past year, right? But now that you're retired, you're released from the captain–vice-captain relationship. So I think *you* can make a proposal to *him* now.'

Ken-chan set the Campus notebook in front of me.

'Open the middle right drawer. I've stocked it with permanent markers, pens, coloured pencils and all kinds of other writing tools. Feel free to use them. Normally I'd suggest a stationery set, paper and an envelope, or some other product for delivering a message like that, but I don't think there's a better choice for your situation than a Campus notebook.'

I stared at the blue cover of the new notebook before me.

Before I knew it, I had stood up and was saying, 'Please let me buy it. I appreciate the gesture, but I don't think I can be confident enough to give it to Takumi if I don't pay for it.'

'Are you sure . . . ? I think Ryoko will get mad at me and say I forced it on you . . .' His tone was suddenly so weak, I had to laugh.

'Don't worry, I'll explain everything to Ryoko-chan!'

Letters from the Ginza Shihodo Stationery Shop

'Then you can pay downstairs on your way out.' Ken-chan bowed briefly and went back to the ground floor.

Once I was alone, I moved the new notebook up and to the left and drew the tenth notebook near to me. Taking slow, deep breaths, I reread Takumi's message on the last page once more. I took my pen case out of my bag, picked up a water-based pen I was used to writing with, and set the tip on the next page.

Looking back at the notebooks starting with number one, I wrote down whatever feelings came up about every aspect of running the club. This time, that time, that other time . . . We had practice every day but Sunday. And Sundays we had practice meets or competitions, so in a year I had fewer than ten days with no plans. I was always with Takumi.

Things that made me happy, things that made me sad, things that frustrated me . . . I'd had so many emotions, but I was so awkward that I'd never once managed to mention them.

Once, on the way home from a practice meet where we got creamed, Takumi said to me, 'We really did badly today . . . I wonder why I can keep trying. I think it's because you keep trying with me, Nanami.'

For a moment, I thought I misheard. He always called me by my last name, Sawamura, but that day he'd called me Nanami.

The subtle closing of that little distance between us was so sudden, I pretended to let it go out the other ear and didn't reply.

'I only keep trying because you keep trying, Takumi.'

I wish I could have been honest and said that. That was my number one regret from the past three years.

Before I knew it, I'd filled over ten pages. When I glanced outside, I saw the sun was sinking – evening was transitioning to night. I took a deep breath.

Notebooks

Dear Captain Takumi Morikawa,

You too! Great work this year. We didn't get very good results at the competition, but I think everyone knows how hard you worked to improve the kyudo club. That's why I think they went along even when you were hard on us or filled the team rosters prioritising talent over grade-level.

I can never go back to them now, but I miss the days drawing my bow with you side by side.

I think if we'd had a lot more time, we could have achieved better results. Next year, or the year after, or maybe the younger students after that – I'm sure it'll happen someday.

So please be proud that you were our captain.

There's no one else who could have done the job.

I'm a little worried that without the kyudo club, the sudden pressure vacuum will land you in bed with a cold or something. I hope you find your next endeavour soon.

It's a mystery that someone as passive and shy as me not only joined a hardcore club like kyudo and stuck with it for three years without quitting, but also served, if only halfway decently, as vice-captain. Everything – everything – is thanks to you, Morikawa-kun. Thank you so much.

Vice-Captain Nanami Sawamura

Having written that much, I took a little yellow sticky note out of my pen case, wrote 'Continued in the next notebook!' on it, and stuck it at the very top of the page.

Then I opened the new Campus notebook to its first page and wrote honestly that I'd liked him ever since we'd met at the open house three years prior.

Letters from the Ginza Shihodo Stationery Shop

Strangely, once I wrote that I liked him – perhaps I was emboldened? – it was easy to continue with, *'Will you be my boyfriend?'* I'm sure the Campus notebook was rooting for me.

Then I wrote:

> *If you can return my feelings, please give this notebook a title and pass it back to me. Yes, just like when we started the practice notes notebook.*
>
> *And leave your last name off, just write Takumi.*
>
> *These three years, I've always wanted to call you 'Takumi'. I want to go from Captain Morikawa-kun and Vice-Captain Sawamura to just Takumi and Nanami.*

'Sorryyy! Didn't mean to be so late! Forgive meee!'

Just as I closed the new notebook, Ryoko-chan came racing up the stairs. Glancing at my phone, I saw it was after six.

'But Rumi will come over! She said you'd eat together at the cafe on your way home.'

'Huh? You called my mum?'

'Yeah. Should I not have? I mean, I'm keeping you so late. And I wanted to have her see Ken-chan for the first time in ages.'

I hurriedly stuffed the eleven notebooks into my bag.

'Um, do you think you could…?'

'Obviously!' said Ryoko-chan, laughing. Ken-chan stood behind her and nodded firmly.

* * *

The people walking down Ginza's alleys in the unseasonable chill were all in a tense hurry. Among them, Ryoko, carrying a

Notebooks

basket and thermos, passed swiftly beneath the swaying willow trees and went into Shihodo. Two others followed her.

'Sorryyy! I'm late again!' Ryoko shouted upon entering.

'Look, I'm not trying to be mean or anything, but Hohozue is only about five minutes from here, so why are you late every time? Is it against your principles to be punctual?' Shihodo's manager, Ken Takarada, voiced his displeasure.

'Sorry, Ken-chan! It's our fault, so don't blame Ryoko-chan,' said Nanami, entering the shop after Ryoko.

'Ahh, Nanami-chan, irasshaimase. It's been about a month, huh? Oh?!' Ken fell silent mid-reply.

'He-hello...' A young man looking valiant in uniform bowed politely.

'This is Takumi Morikawa-kun. Be nice to him, OK?' Nanami blushed bright red.

'Ohh, w-welcome. I'm Ken Takarada of Shihodo. I hope I can be of service to you.'

As the three of them exchanged awkward greetings, Ryoko laid out the sandwich delivery.

'OK, apologies for the wait,' Ryoko called to Ken.

Nanami added, 'Sorry for the wait, Ken-chan. Eat first. Takumi and I will take a look around the shop.' Then she took Takumi's hand and disappeared with him into the notebook section saying, 'Hey, there are tons of different kinds of Campus notebooks. This way, over here!'

'... Good for them, right?' said Ryoko emotionally as she watched them go.

'You played Cupid for two generations, Rumi and now Nanami-chan. So caring!' said Ken as he bit into his sandwich.

'Mmm, I guess...'

Letters from the Ginza Shihodo Stationery Shop

'But maybe it's time to start caring about your own situation?'

Ryoko heaved a sigh and shook her head. 'Yeah, maybe . . .' she grumbled.

At the stationery shop Shihodo in one corner of Ginza, the atmosphere enveloping the two couples' exchanges was gentle and soft.

Postcards

'Dad, are you OK?'

My daughter peered into my face with concern. Well, it was no wonder. I'd just seen my face in the bathroom mirror, and it was white as a sheet.

'Ohh, yeah, I'm fine.' I stood up and let out a sigh. 'Sorry, I don't think I'll stay for the wake tonight. I need some time to calm down and think.'

To Kamisan in her casket, I said, 'See you. See you tomorrow.'

'Are you sure you're OK? You don't have to force it. The memorial address doesn't have to be anything special. If you stress yourself out and ruin your health, it'll be us who suffer for it.'

'You can get us both done with at once! Wouldn't that be convenient?'

My daughter emitted an irritated sigh and shook her head. 'Ran-chan and Jasmine will have none of that. Please just don't overdo it and end up ill in bed. We only invited relatives and close friends, so it'll be a small funeral.'

'What? You didn't invite any of her colleagues?'

'No, Mum said, "It's been over ten years since I retired, so you don't have to invite them." Renting out a huge funeral parlour to have a service with the company would have been a whole thing. She said she didn't want to be a burden.'

'That's your mother for you . . .'

Another sigh slipped out. She was considerate of everyone

Letters from the Ginza Shihodo Stationery Shop

around her to the very end . . . I wondered why she didn't do things how she wanted more often.

'Plus if we had such a fancy funeral, there's no way you would be able to give the memorial address. Her ex-husband? Her number one wish was for you to give the address, you know.'

'I don't get it at all, but if that was her last request of me, then I have no choice. Are you sure you girls are OK with me giving it, though?'

'Yeah. These days, plenty of people cut out the memorial address. It's normal to have the MC read some condolence telegrams and be done. So we're actually going to interpret her wish to make it so you're the only person who reads.'

'. . . I see.'

The wicked hope that my daughters would oppose the idea had flitted across my mind, but it seemed like I had better resign myself to my fate.

I cleared my throat softly and headed for the door. My daughter followed after me, pressing her point.

'Please take it easy as much as you can today and go to bed early. The ceremony starts at 10 a.m., but you should be here by 9 a.m., OK?'

'Mmhmm, got it.'

When I climbed into the taxi I had called to the funeral venue for me, I asked to be taken to the nearest station. The cabbie was a young man. For a moment I thought, *I hope he's not a wild driver*, but he surprised me with his calm, careful work. With a short sigh of relief, I slumped deep into my seat.

Looking up at the sky out of the window as the car took off, I saw it was clear blue without a single cloud. 'A perfect day in Japan even though Kamisan has just died . . .' I murmured to

Postcards

myself. I wouldn't demand a downpour, but it could have at least drizzled.

I suddenly had an idea and said to the driver, 'Sorry, could you head for Ginza?'

He said, 'Huh? Sure, understood. I'll put it into the satnav,' and pulled the car over to input the destination. I took out my phone and called one of the contacts registered in it.

It must have taken about forty minutes? A more seasoned driver would have probably managed it in thirty, but on this day, I appreciated this one's careful handling of the wheel.

'How would you like to pay?'

I took a 10,000-yen note out of my wallet and handed it to him. 'Please keep the change.'

The young driver must have been surprised. Flustered, he said, 'It's too much!'

'It's fine. Please keep it.'

Leaving the grateful taxi driver behind, I exited the car onto the willow-lined lane. Perhaps he had been standing by at the door? Ken-chan, the manager of Shihodo Stationery, came outside.

'Ahh, Ken-chan. Sorry for the short notice.'

'Not at all. Irasshaimase.'

I suppose it had been a month since I'd seen him? The previous time it was about the *nengajo* I ordered from him each New Year's. But I had to think about what to do about those now, too. My custom was to receive the freshly printed cards each November and take the time to add a short handwritten greeting on each one. *But what to do this year?* Usually you'd hold off on New Year's greetings if there were a death in the family... Sure, it'd been decades since the divorce, but my ex-wife had just died. Could I blithely send them out anyhow?

I went through the glass door Ken-chan held open for me and entered the shop. Normally I'd browse the ground floor, checking out the seasonal postcards and new writing utensils, but as could be expected, I wasn't really in the mood that day.

Once the door was closed, Ken-chan turned to face me and bowed deeply.

'I'm so sorry for your loss. Please accept my condolences.'

'Thanks. Agh, it really hits me . . . once someone says those words . . .'

'I-I'm sorry.' Ken-chan dropped his head again.

'No, no, nothing for you to apologise for. I'm just upset to an out-of-character degree.' Then I walked towards the back of the shop. 'Can I go upstairs?'

Normally I'd go straight up, the privilege afforded someone who'd been a patron of the shop for over half a century, but today, I'd arrived so suddenly that I felt like maybe I should ask permission.

'Of course. There aren't any workshops today, so you'll have it all to yourself.'

'I appreciate it. Though so many of the instructors who use this space are pretty ladies. It's a pity I won't be able to see any of them.' I forced a joke, but maybe because I wasn't quite my usual self, Ken-chan's expression remained firm. I shook my head and began climbing the stairs.

As always, I stopped on the landing and looked out over the sales floor. Without even realising it, I murmured, 'Things are the same as always here . . . I'm glad.'

'What are you glad about?' Ken-chan must have caught the last part.

Postcards

'Hm? Oh, nothing important. I guess I was just thinking that the atmosphere of the shop hasn't changed. And it was kind of a relief? We tend to casually assume that this place is like this, that person does that, but I've been realising once again that that isn't the case.'

'Ahh...'

Yes, for me at that moment, a lack of change was what made me the most grateful.

I took a seat in the chair on the landing and looked at the coffee table beside it. A bright red rose stood in a single-flower vase. He must have just put it there that morning; each and every petal was asserting itself with dignity.

Lightly fingering the petals, I nodded. 'Really, I'd like to sit here and drink a cup of tea, gaze absentmindedly out of the window, but I can't today. Gotta draft that pain-in-the-neck memorial address.'

Ken-chan replied with a small, silent nod.

The blinds were up on the first floor, and the rays of sun coming in past the surrounding buildings were so bright. Towards the back on the right was a raised area of about four and a half tatami mats. Opposite that, on the left by the window, was a desk so old you could call it the owner of the shop.

I approached the desk directly and sat on the chair's sturdy cushion. Ken-chan followed and opened one of the drawers lining the left-hand wall from floor to ceiling and took out a box. It was filled with the writing materials I had the shop keep for me.

'I checked on your ink the moment you phoned. I think it will be fine. Will your usual paper do?' Ken-chan asked as he set the box on the desk.

Letters from the Ginza Shihodo Stationery Shop

'Yes, as long as the copyist can read it, I'm good, right?'

'Yes, the copyist is a pro, so you can use whatever you want.'

'I see. Then the paper I'm used to will be good enough.'

'Yes. Though actually I think it's rare for people to submit a handwritten manuscript these days. If you like, I can type it up for you, Sho-chan. Of course, in that case, I'd have to discuss the contents with you . . .'

'Ah . . . hmm. To be honest, I wasn't sure I could write it on my own, so I'd appreciate having your help. What about the shop, though?'

'It'll be fine. I called Ryoko. She said it's slow at Hohozue today, so she'll come with a delivery and stay till evening to watch the shop. She should be here with coffee soon.'

Ken-chan moved my box to the corner of the desk before going back to the wall and taking a laptop and mouse out of a different drawer. Then he released the casters on one of the worktables and rolled it over. Sitting across the table from me, he plugged in the laptop, looked me in the eye, and nodded.

'OK, I'm ready.'

I straightened up, put my hand on the top of the desk, and stroked it lightly with my fingers, sensing the uneven expression of its wooden surface.

'. . . Hmm.'

Where should I start? I was thinking when my mouth began talking on its own, telling the story of how I met Kamisan.

I met Kamisan in Singapore. I had just established a little import–export company using my personal connections and money I had saved; I was thirty years old.

Kamisan worked at the shop at the hotel where I stayed.

Postcards

She was fluent in English, Malay and Mandarin, so I thought at first that she was Singaporean. She was a girl with a round face and an adorable smile.

Back then, international travel wasn't so common, and clients would be delighted to get postcards from business trip destinations, so I was at that store all the time buying them. Apparently she thought I was an oddball for buying nothing but postcards every day.

Once while she was putting my purchases into a paper bag, she said to me, 'Who do you send all these to?' I was surprised to suddenly hear her speak Japanese.

'You speak Japanese?' I replied with a question without answering hers.

Holding back the laughter of a child whose prank has been found out, she blushed and nodded. 'My mother's Japanese.'

'Really? Huh.'

'So who are you sending them to? You buy five or six a day! I bet you're sending them to different ladies all over the place. You must be a naughty man,' she said, looking me straight in the eye. That very moment, I thought, *I'm done for*. I knew I would fall for her.

'What are you talking about? These are for my clients in Japan – they double as notes to say, "I'm working hard in Singapore!" If the company president is out of the country for months on end, people probably start to worry if the company is doing all right, so I send postcards partially as proof that I'm actually working.'

'So that's why you want the most Singapore-looking ones.'

'Yes, exactly. And then I paste a Singaporean stamp on it, and if I take it to the post office, they'll stamp the postmark on

Letters from the Ginza Shihodo Stationery Shop

it, right? In the case of a postcard. There's no cheaper and more fantastic proof than this.'

'Hmm, is that right . . . ? Oh, wait, did you just call yourself the company president?' She suddenly seemed to notice.

It was an awfully rude question, but strangely, I wasn't offended. Plus, I was baby-faced and had only just turned thirty, so I possessed none of the presence you'd expect; even in Japan it was hard to get people to treat me like a company president, so her scepticism wasn't a surprise.

'Well, yes . . . It's just a tiny import–export company – including me on the roster, we have just enough employees to form a baseball team.'

I took my business cards out of my pocket and handed one over. On the front in vertical Japanese, it said, 'Ohashi Trading Ltd. Representative Director and President Shotaro Minatogawa' and the same title was on the back in English.

'Wow, what a business card. I heard Japan lost the war and had a hard time, but I guess it recovered to the point that young company presidents can have nice business cards like these.'

'Well, I'm bending over backwards to get them made at a venerable stationery shop in Ginza, Tokyo, Japan's most prosperous commercial district. As you said, I'm young, so it's hard to get people to trust me. I have to splurge on anything I give to a potential client.'

'Wait, your company is called Ohashi Trading, but you're Minatogawa-san?'

'Yes, "Ohashi" with the characters for "big" and "bridge" because I want to connect the world like one. Some people notice, like you, and sometimes they remember me for my eccentricity. Basically, I didn't think using my own family name would be a good idea.'

Postcards

'Hmm, so you put a lot of thought into it, huh?' she said before returning the card I'd just given her. 'This is wasted on me, so I'll give it back. You don't have any to spare, right? As long as I know you're Minatogawa-san, that's good enough for me.'

'Ack, how embarrassing . . . I'll hurry up and become more successful so you can accept a business card with no reservations,' I said, taking back the card.

She wrote her name on a memo pad and added a phone number, too.

'You can call me Fujiko. That's what all the Japanese people call me.'

'Fujiko-chan? Then please call me Sho-chan. Is that your home number?'

She frowned a bit and shook her head. 'No, the shop's number. My father throws a fit when a man calls the house. If anything comes up, call this number.'

Just then another customer showed up and she started assisting him in English. She spoke pretty Queen's English, a world of difference between that and my broken American English. She gave me a little wink as I left the shop. After that, I was obsessed.

I went to the shop again the next day. After all, I had the excuse of buying postcards, so it was easy to keep returning. When I went in, she greeted me with a 'Morning' or 'Hello' in Japanese from the get-go. She spoke to everyone else in English, so it seemed like I was getting special treatment, which felt nice.

About three days after the business card conversation, I went to the shop first thing in the morning and invited her to dinner.

'I appreciate the invitation, but I have a curfew . . . And the family eats dinner together as a rule. If I just have to eat dinner with a friend, they tell me to invite them over. It's embarrassing, but I've never had dinner at a restaurant with a man. Lunch at a cafe back in high school is as far as I've got.'

So she's the sheltered daughter of a quite strict family, I thought.

'Then how about we go for lunch together on your break?'

'My break doesn't come at a set time. Is that OK?'

'Sure. I'm the company president, after all.'

That is, I tooted my own horn, but I was on a solo business trip, so if I arranged my meetings accordingly, I could do whatever I wanted.

So it was that Kamisan and I became the kind of friends who had lunch together according to her break schedule. I got to know her bit by bit, and was able to let her know me, too, but her lunch break was only sixty minutes. The time we could spend having a relaxed conversation was only ever half an hour or thereabouts. It was always so frustrating that just as things were getting really fun, we'd run out of time; I could never wait for the next day.

Somehow or other we grew closer, but by the time calling each other Fujiko-chan and Sho-chan started to feel cozy instead of too forward, my business trip was coming to an end. The day before I was due to return to Japan, I told her, 'I have to go back to Japan. I'm leaving on tomorrow's boat.'

With sorrow still in her eyes, she put on a broad smile.

'I thought it was a pretty long business trip – a whole month – but now that it's over it felt like no time at all. Did work go well?'

'Yes, thanks. I was able to make all the deals I came to make. Once I get back to Japan, I need to send out the products according to the contracts. And I left all the domestic business up to my

Postcards

employees while I was gone, so I have to make sure no trouble has come up. While I was here I could eat a leisurely lunch with you, but when I get back to Japan, it'll be back to grabbing five minutes to scoff down soba noodles every day.'

'You didn't actually have time to eat lunch with me here, either, did you? I'm sorry I made you go out of your way. But it was fun. Thanks.'

I took her hand.

'What are you saying? I'm the one who pressured you with the invite. I'm the one who should be thanking you – thanks. I want to give you a token of my gratitude. What would you like? I'll be here again in three months, so I'll bring it with me.'

She put her other hand over my hand and said, '. . . Nothing. I don't want anything. If you're doing well, that's enough for me.'

I thought for sure she'd ask for some cosmetics or electronics, so I was caught off guard.

'You really don't need anything?'

'No. As long as you come back in three months happy and healthy, that's enough for me.'

Having built my company with that hungry entrepreneur mindset, her reply felt refreshing. And that was it for me: I was in love.

When I continued holding her hand in silence, unsure what to say, she patted my hand and nodded emphatically. 'Oh, I just had a great idea. So can I ask you for one thing?'

'Sure, anything you like.'

Staring into my eyes, she said, 'OK, then please send me postcards. It doesn't have to be every day. How about . . . hmm, once a week? So that's about twelve in three months. You said you'll be going on business trips around Japan, too, right?

Letters from the Ginza Shihodo Stationery Shop

I'm sure there are all sorts of postcards, even just in Tokyo, and then Osaka, Kyoto and Hokkaido and . . . Kyushu, was it? I've never seen any of the places you told me about. I'd be really happy if you'd send postcards.' Having said that, she ripped a page out of her datebook and wrote an address for me.

'OK, got it. I'll choose pretty ones and be sure to send them.'

And then we kissed for the first time in the comfortable breeze.

'It's a nice story, but aren't you embellishing a bit?' Ken-chan said, his fingers stopping on the keyboard.

'Not even a little. If I were talented enough to come up with a scenario like that, I'd have made a film studio instead of running around in the import–export business. In any case, back then I was so inexperienced, I was desperate to get her attention.'

'Huh, knowing what you're like, I find that hard to believe. By the way, those business cards you mentioned, were they made here?'

'Yes, that's right. Once the company got bigger, your grandfather Kensui-san came to tell me he couldn't handle the contract for all the employees, so I stopped ordering them. I think it was right about the time we topped three hundred employees. They were fine business cards made with high-quality paper and printed on a letterpress; no matter who I handed them to, the recipients' faces would make an "oh!" of surprise. Kensui-san's business cards gave me such a leg up.'

'It's been a long time since we stopped printing, but the press and type are in the basement. I would like to get it spruced up and start doing business cards on a small scale again . . .' Ken-chan said with a nod, a hand on his chin.

'By all means, I hope you will. I'll be looking forward to it!'

Postcards

'So did you send the postcards as you promised?'
'Of course!'

Yes, I sent postcards from the stops on the way back to Japan – Ho Chi Minh, Macau, Hong Kong and so on – and I sent another when I arrived in Yokohama. We have that concept of a three-day monk to describe someone who can't stick with something, but if you can keep something up for four days, it's pretty easy to make it a habit, and after returning to Japan, I made it my daily routine to buy a postcard while out in the afternoon and write on it about what had happened that day, like a journal, before I went to bed.

Up to that point, I had been getting plastered every night, but the thought that I needed to write a postcard to Kamisan caused my drinking pace to slow naturally, and I didn't let myself go anymore. Thinking back, I imagine the only thing that saved my liver when I was single was having this postcard habit.

Back then I was going on lots of business trips to the Kansai area – Osaka, Kyoto, Nara and so on – so lots of the postcards were of things like Osaka Castle, Kinkakuji and the giant Buddha at Todaiji, clearly marketed towards sightseers. They were blatantly touristy and unsophisticated, but I thought Kamisan might like them since she had never seen Japan. That said, I can't believe I got away without any divine punishment while writing stuff like, 'I love you' and, 'Can't wait to see you again', on the back of a picture of the Buddha.

I sent her quite a few from Hokkaido, Kyushu, Shikoku and other regions, too. And of course I sent her pretty much all the major sites from Tokyo: Kaminarimon at Asakusa, Nijubashi at the Imperial Palace and so on.

Letters from the Ginza Shihodo Stationery Shop

Between this and that, the three months passed in no time. I finalised my departure from Japan a couple of weeks ahead of time so I could send a postcard telling her the date that I would arrive in Singapore.

After the several days' voyage, when I stepped off the boat at the end of my journey, Kamisan was standing on the other side of immigration control. The way I felt at that moment is simply indescribable.

The harbour was a chaotic crowd, but the throngs of people disappeared from my view; I could only see her. I abandoned my trunk full of samples, contracts and other important items and ran to her. She ran to meet me and jumped into my arms. We embraced and remained like that for a few moments, unable to move.

On that trip, I had two of my employees with me, so they witnessed us reunite, of course, and for a while after that, the ribbing was intense. 'It was like a scene from a movie!' they said.

That night, Kamisan and I went out for dinner for the first time, and we stayed together until morning.

'Hmm, I get how your employees felt. It really does sound like a movie.' Ken-chan shook his head in amazement.

'Well, I suppose . . . But if you make a face like that at this point in the story, it's hard to keep going.' When I scratched the back of my head self-consciously, Ken-chan couldn't help but laugh.

'OK, please tell me what happened next.'

Business on the second Singapore trip went smoothly, and on our lunch date the day before my return to Japan, Kamisan said

Postcards

to me, 'Hey, you should come to my house tonight. My father said to invite you to dinner.'

That afternoon, I finished up work early, took a thorough shower, put on my best suit, and headed for the hotel lobby. I thought it would be good to bring some kind of gift, but I didn't want to risk bringing the wrong thing, not knowing her father's tastes, so I decided against it. And in the end, that wasn't a bad call.

I was heading down to the lobby a few minutes before we were due to meet when I spotted Kamisan there waiting in an outfit so chic she looked like a different person. I stopped on the stairs and stared, entranced. She looked so pretty I just wanted to stand there gazing at her. Maybe she felt my eyes on her – she waved.

'Hey, sorry I kept you waiting. You're even prettier than usual tonight – makes me nervous to even approach.'

'Ew, I don't need that kind of blatant flattery,' she said with a laugh as she put a red rose through the buttonhole on my jacket.

'What's this for?'

'Oh, you don't know? I'm sure you don't have a dinner jacket with you. But if you put a flower here like this, even a business suit can look more festive. OK, let's go.'

She took my arm and we left the hotel. A large car had been parked in the porte-cochere and a uniformed driver was waiting with the door open.

'What's this car?'

'It's my father's. He let me borrow it to pick you up.'

Kamisan let me get in first and then climbed in after me before saying in English, 'Go ahead.'

The car drove leisurely down the coastal road.

Letters from the Ginza Shihodo Stationery Shop

'We're a little early so I thought I'd take you on a detour to enjoy the sunset over the water.'

The driver said something in Malay with a chuckle. Kamisan blushed bright red and shot something back. They were both talking pretty quickly, so I couldn't follow.

'Jimmy said, "Given the beautiful sunset, I'll overlook it if you want to hold hands. I won't tell your father." He's totally teasing us.'

The elderly chauffeur grinned as he drove.

'Jimmy's been driving for Dad since before I was born. He's never caused an accident, and during the war he protected Dad whenever the situation seemed liable to turn dangerous. He's really important to our family. And he says he approves of you!'

He must have been showing some kindness after noticing I was stiff-as-a-board nervous. A little of the tension went out of my shoulders.

Before long, we had veered from the coastal road onto a mountain road. Partway along we passed a gatepost that stood like a large stone monument, but after that we didn't encounter any other cars.

'There aren't any cars on this road at all . . .'

There wasn't a single streetlight, so in the dark after the sun went down, it was a bit creepy.

'Oh, that's because we're on my family's land. You saw what was left of the gate, right? The gate itself was blown up during the war. Dad doesn't seem interested in fixing it; he says it makes it easier for the neighbours to pass through. As if we're saying, "Go ahead, you can use this road freely."'

This is what it means to be flabbergasted, I thought. We drove

Postcards

through the forest in silence before the space before us abruptly opened and a colonial-style building leaped into view. The outer walls were white and appeared to be floating in space.

A butler in a morning coat stood in the porte-cochere and opened the car door for us with white-gloved hands. Entering through a set of massive double doors, I was met with a mansion so magnificent it was like the set of a movie.

It's embarrassing to admit, but until that moment, I had no idea that Kamisan was the daughter of Chin-san, the most successful financier in Singapore.

Chin-san met me in a dinner jacket and treated me to a multi-course dinner at a grand table that could have easily seated twenty people. The conversation was entirely in English, and he mainly spoke about art, music and theatre; at the time, I couldn't keep up.

After dinner, Chin-san invited me to his study. Kamisan looked worried, so I gave her a light-hearted wink as I went. When we got to his study, he offered me a cigar and handed me a glass of whisky on the rocks.

Once we were comfortably seated, Chin-san got straight to the point. 'So how long have you been seeing my daughter?'

'We met about four months ago. I run a small import–export company in Tokyo and came here on business. So far our relationship has consisted of letters and lunch dates, nothing you would have to be concerned about.'

Obviously I couldn't tell the truth. I took out a business card and handed it to him.

'Ohashi Trading . . . ? I don't mean to be rude, but it's my first time hearing of it.'

Of course he hadn't heard of it. He was the CEO of a major

Letters from the Ginza Shihodo Stationery Shop

corporation, such a giant he was impossible to get a meeting with; it was natural that he hadn't heard of a small company that had only been established for a few years.

I told him how I'd lost my mother and father in the war, cut my teeth selling goods on the black market and used that money to get a college degree, then got a job at a big trading company and went independent after working there for a few years. I honestly admitted it was my second time in Singapore and that I was heading back to Japan on a boat the next day.

Chin-san listened quietly without interrupting me. After hearing what I had to say, he looked me right in the eye and nodded. 'I'm sure you'll succeed in business. It's just a hunch, but my intuition is almost never wrong. In exchange, though, you'll be preoccupied with your passion for work and probably won't be able to build a peaceful family life. This may be biased, but having lost your parents early, you sadly do not know what a family is. By which I mean, you grew up without understanding what a father and a mother should be. So I imagine that you and my daughter are looking for different things in a home. Therefore, I'm sorry, but please just be friends with Fujiko. Frankly, I'd like you to not see her again.'

There was nothing I could say in reply. During my twenties I'd experienced my share of relationships with the opposite sex, but as Chin-san said, I had always prioritised work. As a result, I'd never made it as far as marriage.

'You don't care how she feels?' I asked, unsure of how else to react, but he shook his head.

'I feel I entertain most of her whims. When she wanted to go to school, I let her go; when she said she wanted to work, I allowed it, and I turned a blind eye to the fact that she chose to

Postcards

work somewhere with no family connections. But the natural progression of relationships with the opposite sex is marriage, and I need her to choose someone who is appropriate for the Chin family. I'm sorry, but though you have the potential to be a great businessman, you haven't achieved enough for me to offer you my daughter. Of course, if you want to be adopted into my family, that's a different story. Though in that case, you'd have to settle your company's accounts and prepare to be buried in Singapore.'

With that, he stood up as if to say the conversation was over and dropped the needle of the phonograph by the window. Before long, a piano sonata filled the room at a muted volume. I bowed deeply and took my exit.

In the hallway, Kamisan was waiting. Surprisingly, she had changed from her dinner dress into a casual outfit, like she was about to leave on a trip.

When we went outside holding hands, Jimmy was waiting for us. He had also changed from his uniform into an informal shirt and jeans. The car, too, wasn't the luxury vehicle he'd picked us up in, but an old Chevrolet. I got into Jimmy's car as told and then Kamisan whispered into my ear.

'Run away with me. I'll go with you to Japan.'

I would have yelped in surprise, but she plugged my mouth with a kiss. Jimmy let out a low whistle and purposely wobbled the steering wheel.

'Jimmy was kind enough to let us use his own car. You wouldn't want to elope in my dad's car, right?'

Exiting the pitch-dark driveway, we came out onto the coastal road to find a white moon shining brilliantly in the sky.

Letters from the Ginza Shihodo Stationery Shop

'Jimmy says, "Regardless of what your father says, the moon is celebrating you two."'

I splurged on a first-class cabin for the trip back to Japan. I heard later that the Chin family was in an uproar over Kamisan's disappearance, though Chin-san himself was apparently self-possessed and simply refused to engage, saying, 'Leave her be.' Maybe he thought she would be back at some point.

The first-class voyage was truly elegant and enjoyable. Thinking back now, it was the one and only time I showed Kamisan how important she was to me. Back then, the culture of travelling on luxury passenger ships was still extant in Europe, especially, and the evening meal was the real deal, to the point that a dinner jacket was required. There was even a tailor on board, and I had my first dinner jacket made for me on that trip.

Once we arrived in Japan, I just forced her to help with work. I didn't let her have a normal married life. Kamisan was skilled with languages and, as one might expect of Chin-san's daughter, she had a good grasp of essential business principles. For those reasons, I had her take over sales in Asia. That meant that our relationship as manager and employee was stronger than that of husband and wife. She didn't seem to dislike working, so I took advantage and delegated more and more responsibilities to her.

Even so, we were young, and the year after we married, our eldest daughter was born. The very next year, Kamisan was pregnant with our second daughter. But I pushed all the childcare duties onto her and threw myself even harder into work. Or rather, I ran away into it.

I have almost no memories of living with my father. As a

Postcards

result, I had no idea how a father was meant to behave with his family. In other words, it was exactly as Chin-san had observed.

When I went home, my wife and the girls were there waiting for me, but I had no idea what to talk to them about. In the end, I just droned on to Kamisan about work. Now I realise I should have inquired more about the girls. I didn't even think to ask, 'What did you get up to today?'

Despite that, she handled everything at home while continuing to work without ever once complaining. I think she was just very capable to begin with, but at the time, our finances were in fairly good shape as well, so we were able to hire a nurse and other staff. We received a lot of help from other people.

'Hmm, it's like a rapid economic growth era tale of success combined with a youthful love story. But if your wife was so talented, why did you split up? It was such a grand romance that you eloped!'

'. . . Mm, there's not really anything I can say. How to put it? I guess when you're a disappointing guy like me, it's hard to have a partner who is too perfect.'

In the midst of all that, me paying no attention to my family and demanding the impossible at the office, Kamisan found out I was involved with another woman. It must have been about eight years into our marriage? But she didn't say a thing. She smiled and treated me the same as normal, both at home and at work. That hit me hard, given the way I was back then.

In the end, I asked her for a divorce when our younger daughter entered elementary school. She resisted quite forcefully, but she eventually stamped her seal on the document; the last time we took a photo as the four of us was in front of that elementary school entrance ceremony sign.

Next she announced, 'I'm quitting the company.' Now that was a problem for me. I mean, she was a director-level executive as the head of Asia, and I had her managing over one hundred employees.

The day she resigned as director, a bunch of old-guard execs and other employees gave me hell. 'You should be the one quitting!' they said. And they were right, so I couldn't say a thing.

That happened when I was thirty-eight, and it was rough, so I decided I would never get married again. But I did, at age forty – to a woman named Ran. Yes, two names with flower kanji in a row. Fujiko had been three years my junior, but Ran was a whole twelve years younger than me.

I had learned my lesson with Kamisan, so I didn't let Ran have anything to do with my business. For that reason, my employees naturally called her Okusan. The old-hand execs and other employees said, 'It wouldn't feel right to call a different person your *kamisan*.' Well, I could understand their urge to say something that would sting.

I heard later from Okusan that before we officially tied the knot, Kamisan had gone out of her way to contact her.

'Sho-chan is a good person, but he's nice to *everyone*. Put simply, he's loose with women. Of course, he knows how to do his job and makes decent money, but as a husband and father, he's the worst. Is that all right with you?'

Apparently that's what she said the moment they met. But when she saw that Okusan had made up her mind, she said, 'OK, I understand. Then congratulations,' and promptly presented her with a wedding gift envelope containing a surprisingly large amount of money. And then she said, 'If you ever need help, talk to me. Let's be friends. I don't have any relatives in Japan, so please be my little sister.'

When I heard that story I was so impressed. *Agh, she's a far bigger person than me.* I don't think most people would be able to do such a thing.

Incidentally, Kamisan used the divorce settlement as capital to purchase a small cosmetics company. Her business model – cosmetics made by women from natural ingredients without chemical additives, sold by women – was a success, and she's grown it into one of Japan's leading global brands. Now I know that she was more than a cut above me as a business person as well.

As if to remedy the failure of my first marriage, I made an effort to spend more time at home whenever possible. Perhaps, as a result, I had two daughters a year apart with Ran as well. I found it strange that I only ever had girls, but one of my good friends told me, 'Men who make women cry will only produce daughters.' I got the message and couldn't say a word in reply.

The first five years or so went fine, and I thought, *The idea that you can use your failures to grow future success really can be applied in any arena.* But there was a period at that time during which I got busier and busier; I listed the company, was opening more branches both domestically and overseas, and so on. Entertaining and being entertained, I ended up with a vigorous night life at the clubs . . . And eventually, at age forty-seven, I got divorced for the second time.

Kamisan showed up, which made it really rough. During her own divorce she had maintained composure despite brimming with silent anger, but for some reason this time she gave me the fiercest scowl.

Letters from the Ginza Shihodo Stationery Shop

I was summoned to a hotel near my work, and when I went over, I found Kamisan waiting for me clad in a Chanel suit. She was pretty, but it was as if furious flames were flickering behind her, and I was truly terrified. Ever since the divorce, whenever she heard a bad rumour about me or the company, she would summon me for a lecture, but this time was a whole other level, to the point that despite the chilly air-conditioning in the hotel lounge, I could feel the sweat rolling down my back.

Incidentally, though my employees didn't really react to my second divorce, the daughters I'd had with Kamisan gave me awfully icy glares. I don't have any siblings, and Kamisan's siblings weren't in Japan, so naturally the girls had no cousins. Perhaps that was part of the reason that Kamisan's daughters seemed to have built cousin-like relationships with Okusan's daughters.

Having skedaddled out of two marriages, I threw myself into work all the more, singing the praises of the single life. The company was flush with cash, and it was the bubble era, so we scaled up at a tremendous speed. But there is indeed many a slip between the cup and the lip, and my health failed me. It was fairly depressing given that I thought my only strong point was my robustness. But if I hadn't gotten sick, I might have bankrupted my company.

Due to my illness, there were limitations on how much I could work, so I was forced to walk away from a number of investment deals. Resort development, a golf course, taking over a foreign mining company – any of them would have been a massive investment. At the time, banks' loan screenings were lax, and you could borrow multiple times your company's gross yearly sales. If you thought about it clearly, you'd realise right away that it was shady, but at the time no one noticed, and no one tried to notice.

Postcards

The bubble burst while I was in hospital and we entered what are now called the 'lost' two – or sometimes three – decades. Since my company didn't take on any absurd liabilities, but instead just continued with the business I'd been cultivating for many years – that of buying and selling actual products – I managed to escape without putting any of my employees in difficult circumstances. On the contrary, we actually expanded because so many of our competitors went bankrupt or closed down and we took over their business. You never know what will end up being good luck.

The nurse who was in charge of my sick room during that period became my third wife. I was precisely fifty. She told me her name was Jasmine. Fujiko, Ran and then Jasmine. *There must be something connecting me to women with flower names*, I thought.

She was a student from the Philippines who had come to study nursing in Japan. I was chosen as her charge because of all the patients, I was the best at English, and she didn't know much Japanese. It's odd, when you think about it . . . I guess it was about six months of this somewhat strange daily life? Me the ageing patient, speaking English out of consideration for a young nurse. At first we only exchanged the formalities that patients and nurses do, but we soon became friends across the age gap, and as her Japanese improved, we fell in love.

She was over two trips around the Chinese zodiac younger than me, the same age as my eldest daughter with Kamisan. I thought this would surely earn me some icy looks from my four daughters, but to my surprise, they were happy for us. I think Kamisan and Okusan must have had something to do with that.

I called my first wife Kamisan and my second wife Okusan, so I decided to call my third wife Waifu. As she was born in the Philippines, I figured the English might be easier for her to understand.

So it was that I got married for the third time, but in the end, I just wasn't cut out for marriage, and it was at age sixty that I got divorced for the third time. Kamisan and Okusan stood by Waifu's side during the divorce negotiations, so I waved the white flag from the get-go. My lawyer got frustrated and said, 'You don't have to do *everything* they say . . .' That's how badly I lost the will to fight.

I just wanted to feel better as soon as I could, even if I ended up flat broke. And it was then that I decided, *No matter what else happens, I'm staying single till I die.*

'Sorry I'm late . . .' came a kind voice abruptly from the bottom of the stairs. I knew right away who it was.

'Oh, Ryoko-chan. Hello!'

It seemed she had come to bring us coffee.

'Hey, thanks. What do you think? Would you like to take a break?' said Ken-chan.

'Hmm, sure, let's take a little break.'

I stood up from my seat and stretched. Ryoko-chan put the wicker basket and coffee pot she brought over on one of the worktables and approached me to bow deeply.

'Sho-chan, I'm so sorry for your loss. Please accept my condolences.'

'. . . Thanks.' I straightened up and bowed my head.

'Where should I set up?' Ryoko-chan asked, and Ken-chan pointed to the raised area.

'Over there, please.'

'OK,' she replied and then moved the wicker basket to the

Postcards

edge of the raised area. The space beneath was a drawer, and she opened it to take out a low folding table and cushions.

'Let me give you a hand.'

Ken-chan took the table, unfolded the legs, and set it on the raised area. Seeing them working together so harmoniously warmed my heart somehow.

Ryoko-chan laid out the cushions and draped a white cloth she produced from the basket over the table. She set out cups, saucers, small plates and forks, followed by a sugar bowl and a creamer of milk, plus a napkin holder filled with plenty of paper napkins. Lastly, she put out a tray with moist towels. The place was rapidly equipped like a full-service outpost of the cafe Hohozue.

After moving the basket and coffee pot to the most humble seat at the table, Ryoko-chan stepped off from the raised area.

'There's a snack in there from the owner. "Because I'm sure Sho-chan says he can't get anything down and is drinking like a fish in the meantime," he said. Anyhow, I'll be downstairs minding the shop. Be a good help to Sho-chan, OK, Ken-chan?'

'Will do. Thanks.' Ken-chan answered gently. I straightened up and bowed to Ryoko-chan.

'Thanks. I'm sure it will be delicious. Tell your dad "hi" for me.'

'Oh yeah, I'm sure you have a lot going on now, but once things calm down, please stop by the cafe.'

'I'll do that. Though I do see your dad in Yushima now and then.' I gestured striking a ball with a cue. There was a pool hall we frequented in Yushima.

'I thought you might! When the weather's bad and there aren't many customers, he says, "I'm going out for a bit," and doesn't come back for half a day. I figured it was pool, and sure enough.' Then she said, 'OK, see you later,' and went downstairs.

Once Ryoko-chan was out of sight, I sat on the raised area to take off my shoes and then went onto the tatami. I felt less tense, which was a relief.

'I'm a customer today so I'll help myself to the seat of honour,' I commented as I lowered myself onto the cushion at the far end of the table. Ken-chan sat down after I was settled.

'By the way, Ken-chan, how long are you planning on leaving Ryoko-chan hanging?' I asked the question that had been on my mind for a while without mincing words. It seemed to catch him off guard, and he fumbled for an answer.

'. . . I'm not leaving her hanging or anything. We're just friends, like we have been since we were kids.'

'Hmm, if you say so. A fine young lady like that is bound to be getting invitations from all sorts of people, and her dad says she's even been proposed to. Make sure someone doesn't snatch her from under your nose.' I felt like I might be being a bit harsh, but I said it anyway.

'Mmhmm . . .' Ken-chan answered vaguely as he took cake boxes out of the basket and opened the lids to show me. There was one eclair and one cream puff, plus two firm, oven-baked puddings.

'Ooh, looks delicious,' I said instinctively. I was moved by the owner's concern.

'The eclair for you, Sho-chan? Or would you like a cream puff for a change?'

'Hmm, the cream puff looks delectable, but yeah, today I'd like the eclair.' It suddenly hit me that the topic had changed. 'To get back to what we were saying: Ryoko-chan is a choice that would put my mind at ease too. You can be a bit of a scatterbrain

Postcards

and I think she'd be a great support to you. Well, I know I'm being nosy, but . . . you should really have a proper think on it.'

'. . . Mmhmm,' he answered vaguely as he handed me a plate with the eclair.

'Don't mind if I do!' I said before grabbing the eclair and taking a huge bite. Then I took a sip of the coffee he'd just poured for me, black. '. . . So good, right?'

Ken-chan replied with a little nod, picked up his cream puff, and took a huge bite like me. For a little while, we just ate our pastries and drank our coffee. I was grateful that he was willing to simply sit in silence with me.

Having regained some energy from the eclair and coffee, a thought entered my mind. It came out of my mouth as words before I was even conscious of it.

'. . . I was just thinking . . . I told you all those stories, but . . .' I wiped my sticky hands on a moist towel and then straightened up to face Ken-chan. 'Maybe standard is best for the memorial address?'

Ken-chan looked at me with some surprise.

'If I write something chock-full of my feelings, it's embarrassing, you know? Especially with Okusan and Waifu there, and my daughters, it'd be a bit . . . I feel bad for saying this after all the time you've spent with me on this, but . . .'

'No need to worry about that. But are you sure a standard address is what you want?'

I just said, 'Yeah.' Even I was surprised by how weak I sounded.

Ken-chan looked like he wasn't quite sure how to proceed. Then he said, 'One second,' and went to get the computer from the worktable.

'So, a normal address would start with something like,

Letters from the Ginza Shihodo Stationery Shop

"So-and-so-san, you've departed ahead of me",' he said, showing me a few sample sentences.

We looked at various examples on different websites. Then I chose two that were neither overly formal nor too casual and asked him to mix and match them into one.

'You really want something this conventional? What if I customised it a bit? The story of how you met in Singapore is so romantic. I think it'd be good . . .'

'No, no . . . I don't think I could read something like that in front of the portrait of my dead kamisan. Please have them put the hiragana over the kanji. And write big. I can't read small print with my naked eyes, and I don't want to get up there in front of the mic and have to fiddle around with reading glasses.' I forced a smile. The strained expression might have just made me look extra ghoulish.

'Understood. Shihodo has been doing business with the copyists at Tsukushikai for many years, so I'll use them. They've done a number of jobs for you before, and I think we'll probably be able to get the same person to write for you again. They're considerate like that, so you can rest easy.'

'I'm counting on you. Make sure they write everything the standard way, no fancy styling.'

Once, when I was still working, I became the president of an industry group for a while, and the celebratory address I was given was written so fluidly that I struggled with it. There was no pronunciation guide for the difficult characters, so I kept getting stuck as I read – it was so embarrassing. Someone who's never had the experience of drawing a blank on characters you can normally read once you're nervous up in front of a mic can't possibly understand.

'Very well.'

I pulled my wallet out of my jacket.

'I'd hate to forget to pay in the hustle and bustle so let me settle up ahead of time.'

Ken-chan seemed to think for a moment but then immediately said, 'No, that's OK,' shaking his head. 'This is short, so it won't cost very much. You can pay next time you come to the shop.'

'Really? Thanks.'

'No problem. Oh and of course I'll pay Tsukushikai ahead of time, so no need to worry on that score. I'm sure you're most concerned about that part, but such a small amount is no problem for Shihodo.'

'. . . You remembered, huh?'

Back when my company was still small, I had an awfully rough time juggling capital, so whenever I personally pay for something I've made it a habit of settling in cash up front. It was so reassuring that Ken-chan actually remembered the details of my proclivities.

'OK, then, I'll let you handle it.'

'You can count on me. I'll be at the ceremony tomorrow, so I'll deliver it to you there. It starts at 10 a.m., right? I'll make sure to be there by 9:30.'

'Naw, you can cut it closer. If it's just the document you showed me, then I should be fine without rehearsing. I'd feel bad to have you show up too early, so, hmm, yeah, come at 9:55.'

'Understood.'

I drained the rest of my coffee and slipped my feet into my shoes.

'You're not about to go drinking, are you?' Ken-chan called after me.

Letters from the Ginza Shihodo Stationery Shop

'Hmm, what should I do? Oh, speaking of which, good for, uh . . . what was her name? From Fumi-mama's. Oh, right, Yuri-chan.' I remembered his sudden phone call the other day asking me how to get in touch with the owner of Club Fumi.

'Oh, that's right!' Ken-chan put his shoes on and straightened up before bowing his head. 'They managed to work things out, so thank you.'

'If me frequenting clubs could be of use to someone then it wasn't for nothing, right?'

'True, but . . .' The worried look on his face cracked me up.

'Don't worry. Even I'm gonna go straight home today. I'll go to bed early, maybe hop in the bath beforehand.'

'Please do. Oh, I don't mean to give you extra things to carry, but please take the pudding. I'm sure all you have at home is tea and alcohol.' He repacked the boxes, put them in the bag, and handed it to me.

'There are spoons in the boxes. Take the ice packs out when you put them in the fridge.'

'Aw, cheers. Hohozue pudding goes great with brandy.'

'That it does. But you can't overdo it tonight. Tomorrow's a big day.'

I gave him an obedient nod and promptly headed home.

After my bath, I nursed some brandy over a pudding and went to bed, but even though I knew I was tired, my eyes were wide open and I couldn't sleep.

Around the time the date changed over, I started playing old records in the order I recalled them and stared vacantly out of the window. From my room on the second floor, I had a good view of the people coming and going on the street.

Postcards

A young couple holding hands passed by, laughing with mouths wide open, but also, a man and a woman who perhaps had some kind of issue, huddled together with grave looks on their faces. Sighing, I closed the curtains and turned to face the inside of my room.

Not a single picture on the walls nor a single flower in a vase. In the drab room, Bill Evans's piano played softly. My eyes landed abruptly on the one postcard standing on the bookshelf. I'd made it in Kamakura soon after marrying Kamisan. I'd found it by chance in the process of moving to this apartment, and displayed it out of nostalgia.

'Hey, let's get our picture taken.'

Back then, there were roadside photographers at most tourist spots whose business was taking pictures, developing them, printing them, and then sending them.

'If you want a picture, I can take it. You think my camera doesn't have a timer?' I said, but Kamisan shook her head.

'Ugh, no, take a closer look at the sign. It says they'll make you a postcard. I left all my friends and everyone who helped me out in life to come here without telling anyone. I'd at least like to send a marriage announcement.'

That was how we ended up making the postcard.

In the picture, Kamisan was wearing a polka-dot dress with a white collar, and I wore a linen three-piece suit with a boater. It was black and white, but I had no trouble recalling the vibrant blue of her dress. I don't remember how many copies we had them print, but I only had one left. I hugged it close and lay down in bed.

*

Letters from the Ginza Shihodo Stationery Shop

'Sorry I kept you waiting.'

Ken-chan showed up at the venue at 9:50, and when he found me, he handed over a paper bag containing the memorial address.

'Thanks, sorry to put you out.'

I tucked the address into my breast pocket and bowed my head.

'Not at all. See you later,' Ken-chan said, shaking his head, before scurrying away to take a seat at the back of the room. Usually he would chit-chat more, so I thought it was strange.

After the monk finished reading the sutra, it was time for the memorial address. I buttoned my jacket and adjusted my posture.

'Now we'll hear the memorial address. It was the deceased's strong preference to have an old friend, Shotaro Minatogawa-sama, deliver it. Minatogawa-sama, if you please.'

Ushered by a member of the funeral parlour's staff, I approached the mic in front of the altar. On my way up, I bowed to my daughters and the other people attending. I'd been told it would be a small affair, but there were well over two hundred people. It really showed how well-connected Kamisan had been despite officially retiring over ten years ago.

When I stood in front of the mic, Kamisan's portrait was directly opposite me. I'd seen it any number of times since entering the venue, but somehow facing it head-on like this made me nervous.

I opened the envelope Ken-chan had prepared for me and took out the carefully folded address. Putting the envelope back into my pocket, I faced the mic and projected my voice.

'Allow me to . . .'

I had no more words.

Postcards

There was nothing written on the paper, just a big sticky note.

Dear Sho-chan,

I'm sorry. A boiler plate memorial address just wouldn't be like you, and I don't think Kamisan would ever forgive you, either. Please give her a send-off in your own words.

Ken

'... He got me good.' I only remember what I said up until I muttered those words under my breath. All I know is that partway through I started to cry and couldn't stop.

Ken-chan passed by me on his way back from offering incense. He leaned into my ear for a split second to whisper, 'I'm sorry,' before returning to his seat. Really, I would have liked to get a jab in, but having just cried, I couldn't quite find my voice.

'It's time to prepare the casket. We'd like to have you all lay the flowers you brought with the deceased. A staff member will come around with them now, so please take part.'

At the MC's announcement, florists began cutting the stems of flower offerings and handing the blossoms out. The altar that had been crammed with flowers suddenly looked rather lonely, and instead, Kamisan was completely surrounded by blossoms, leaving just her face peeking out from the casket.

'Hey Dad, do you have a second?'

One of my daughters, her eyes puffy and red from crying, tugged on my sleeve. She was holding a tin that looked like it might contain cookies.

Letters from the Ginza Shihodo Stationery Shop

'The memorial address was really good. I think that's the first time I've ever heard how you felt about Mum. And I'm happy I got to hear about what you two were like before we came along. I can't believe you eloped . . . The thought that we were born as the result of such a grand romance made me cry so much.'

'. . . Oh.'

There must have been something else I could have said, but I couldn't think of anything.

'I always thought you liked Ran-chan and Jasmine more than Mum. But that wasn't true. I know now that you really loved Mum, too. I was kind of happy to hear that. Thanks.'

'Oh, I see.'

'So, there's something I want you to see.' She raised the tin she was holding up to eye level. 'Do you know what the first thing was that Mum asked me to do once she had stabilised after being taken to the hospital?'

'Hmm. What was it?'

'She wanted me to bring her this tin. She kept it all the way in the back of her closet. It wasn't easy to dig out. But when I brought it to her, she looked so happy . . . Honestly, I was kind of pissed off. She seemed happier to have this dusty old tin than the flowers we got for her.'

I took a long look at the tin. I couldn't recall ever seeing it before.

'So I asked her, "What's in the tin?" Like, "It was a struggle to get it out for you, so tell me what's inside." Then, despite being pale from her sickness, she suddenly blushed bright red . . . She showed me, but not before saying, "It's a secret. You can't tell anyone. They're my treasures."'

I cocked my head. I had no idea what 'they' might be.

Postcards

'Open it,' said my daughter, offering me the tin. It seemed very old and had dents here and there, some cloudy spots and little scratches.

I lifted the lid to find the photo postcard we'd made in Kamakura. And beneath that were the postcards I'd sent her...

From the ones I'd sent on my way back to Japan – Ho Chi Minh, Macau, Hong Kong – to the Yokohama harbour, Osaka Castle, Kyoto's Kinkakuji, Yasaka Jinja, and shrine maidens, the clock tower and Dr Clark in Hokkaido, Hakata, Naruto's whirlpools, Chinatown and Glover's residence in Nagasaki, Nara's giant Buddha, the view of Kobe at night, Nijubashi at the Imperial Palace, and Tokyo Station... They were all postcards I'd sent to Kamisan.

'She said they're all postcards you sent from Japan to Singapore before you guys got married? Do you remember how many you sent?'

I silently shook my head.

'Ninety-nine. Plus the one you made from the photo in Kamakura to announce your marriage makes one hundred. These were her treasures.' My daughter shook my shoulders. 'So go put them by her heart, with your two hands. I'm sure she would want to take them with her.'

I could tell the people who were still around were looking on warmly. I nodded quietly and approached the casket.

Kamisan's face was peaceful, and she was as beautiful as the first time I met her at the hotel shop. With shaking hands I laid each postcard at her breast one by one. My tears overflowed onto them but were stoutly repelled since I had written the letters in a ballpoint pen using permanent ink so they would survive the trip overseas without bleeding.

Letters from the Ginza Shihodo Stationery Shop

The last postcard was the one we made together in Kamakura. I placed it gently with both hands. Perhaps because my eyes were blurred from the tears, it looked as though she was smiling.

'Hey, how long are you planning on staying there like that?'
'Yeah, you're going to catch a cold.'
I heard the voices of Ran and Jasmine behind me. I realised I was standing in front of the door to the crematorium.
'I'm all right. Leave me be for a little longer,' I answered crankily.
'What are you talking about? You've already cried enough for a lifetime, haven't you? Your voice is so hoarse I can't understand what you're saying,' said Ran in frustration.
'I got so jealous partway through, actually. No offence to Fujiko-san, but I never got a single postcard. I really envy her. So next time you go somewhere, send me a postcard!' said Jasmine, slipping her little finger around mine to unilaterally initiate a pinkie promise.
'Yeah, I never got one either. But I'd rather have a memorial address than a postcard. A memorial address given by your sobbing ex-husband? Like, that really packs a punch! Do one at my funeral, too! I'll never forgive you if you die before me!' said Ran, pinching my cheek.
'Hey, what're you pinching me for?'
'Shush! That was for Fujiko-chan! You're really such an idiot!'
'Right on! Nice one, Ran-chan!'
Then they both piled on in a hug.
'Fujiko-chaaan! Why isn't she here? I miss her!' said Ran, and Jasmine began to sob.
And then, how long did I spend rubbing their backs?
'Are you feeling better?' I asked, and they both nodded.

Postcards

'Ahh, I feel refreshed somehow,' said Ran, and Jasmine nodded. Then she suddenly burst out laughing.

'Ran-chan, your makeup is totally destroyed.'

'That's rich considering you look just as bad!'

They pointed at each other's faces, laughing so hard they were holding their stomachs. Even I found myself laughing. I was sure Kamisan was laughing on her way to heaven, too.

'OK, let's go to the waiting room. If you end up ill in bed because you were standing out here in the freezing cold for too long, Fujiko-chan will be mad at you!'

'Yes, yes! Get it together!'

I set off walking towards the waiting room supported on either side by Ran and Jasmine.

* * *

One day, not long before Christmas, a letter arrived by registered mail at Shihodo Stationery in Ginza.

'Merry Christmas!' the elderly postman said with a grin as he handed it over.

'Yes, indeed, Merry Christmas. You're even on Santa duty now, huh?' Ken Takarada, Shihodo's manager said, smiling as he accepted the letter.

'Pretty soon it'll be New Year's and I'll have to do a lion dance!' the postman quipped before bustling out of the shop.

Ken checked the sender's name and, with a puzzled look on his face, got out a pair of scissors to cut the seal. Inside was an envelope and a paper slip case of the sort that might contain a gift certificate with the English word 'Gift' printed on it.

When he opened the envelope, there was a neatly written letter inside.

Letters from the Ginza Shihodo Stationery Shop

Dear Ken-chan,

Thank you for all your help recently. When I unfolded the memorial address, I thought, 'He got me good,' but it turned out all right in the end, I forgive you.

It must have been an awful speech, all ad lib, but thanks to you, I was able to say a proper goodbye to Kamisan. My daughters and other attendees said, 'You did great! Made me cry!'

Of course, I'm not sure how to feel about getting praised for just talking off the top of my head.

Regardless, it's all thanks to you. You have my gratitude.

This present is a thank-you and payback at the same time. Please accept it – and also make sure you use it.

Unfortunately, I got married three times and divorced three times, but I do believe marriage is a good thing. You should definitely have a go.

Oh, of course I mean you should have a go at marriage, not divorce.

I'm sure you're busy over the New Year's, but once the holiday period is over, please go somewhere with Ryoko-chan.

If you need someone to watch Shihodo, I'll do it. No offence, but I'm confident that I'm a better salesman than you. If you lose sales, I'll make up the difference.

In any case, you shouldn't assume that the people who are important to you will always be there. That's one thing I can say for sure.

If you don't hold on to the important people in your life, they'll be gone.

And if someone important to you chooses to rely on you,

Postcards

please accept your role. You mustn't run away like I did. I made the same mistake three times, so I know what I'm talking about.

It's flu season out there, so please take care of yourself. See you soon.

Shotaro

Inside the slip case was an accommodation voucher for 100,000 yen and a flyer that screamed 'homemade' titled 'Sho-chan's Picks! Recommended Hotels in the Kanto Area'.

Ken chuckled and shook his head lightly.

'Sho-chan, you're such a meddler . . . but thank you.' Just as he murmured this to himself, the poster girl of the cafe Hohozue walked in.

'Ken-chan, this came from Sho-chan . . .'

In Ryoko's hands were a letter and paper slip case much like the ones Ken had received. He pointed at the slip case and said, 'What's inside?'

'This? A travel voucher for 100,000 yen. It says you can use it for planes, boats, trains, buses and even taxis.'

Ken cocked his head and thought for a moment. Before long a little smile appeared on his face.

'I just got this. An accommodations voucher for the same amount, 100,000 yen.'

'What?! Oh, wow!' she said, taking Ken's slip case from his hand and examining the contents.

'Do you think it's OK for us to accept these?'

'Yeah, I mean . . . He did give them to us.'

When Ryoko heard Ken's reply, she beamed and pulled out her smartphone.

Letters from the Ginza Shihodo Stationery Shop

'So where should we go? Or, er, can you close the shop?'

In one corner of Ginza, Tokyo, the manager of Shihodo Stationery and his childhood friend began to close the vague distance between them. The shop was filled with the warmth and affection of the people quietly watching over them.

Memo Pads

'All the cooking equipment is in, so the construction itself is finished. The cleaners are coming this afternoon, and then after one last good check, I'll be able to hand it over to you in the morning as planned,' the site manager said.

'I'm sorry for all my unreasonable requests.' I bowed my head.

'It sure was rough, I'll tell you that,' the manager said with a laugh. 'But it made me feel like you were really keeping an eye on our work. It was hard, but fun at the same time. I'll be a bit sad when this job is over.'

It was only a little counter with eight seats, but to me, it was my first 'castle', so I couldn't help but obsess about every last detail. At the same time, it wasn't as if I had a sponsor, so my funds were limited; it must have been hard for the manager to make it all happen within my budget. I felt bad for pushing him. Every time I stopped by, I brought snacks and drinks, but there was no way that alone would make us even. *I'll have to invite him to the restaurant once it's open*, I thought.

A client hanging around the project site is only ever a bother, so I bowed and took my leave. The manager replied with a casual wave.

When I stepped back onto the street, it was just after 2 p.m. Even the restaurants that served lunch were taking down their *noren* and closing up for their afternoon break before dinner, and there wasn't much foot traffic. Taking my Rhodia Block Memo out of my pocket, I ran my eyes over the notes I'd taken. Given that the restaurant was almost ready, there were hardly any to-dos left. I'd struck a line through each item that was basically finished, and only one remained.

After confirming that, I closed the Rhodia and put it in my pocket. I took out my phone and dialled a number I'd been calling a lot lately.

'Shihodo Stationery!' the manager Takarada-san answered on the third ring.

'Hello, this is Fuda. You were arranging a copyist for me?'

'Yes, of course, Fuda-sama.' Takarada-san sounded a bit surprised.

'Sorry, it's a bit earlier than my reservation, but do you mind if I come over now?'

'Not at all. Your order just came in.'

Hearing that was a relief. I hurried past the willow trees lining the street to the venerable old stationery shop Shihodo with its landmark, the cylindrical red postbox.

'Tatsuo Wanno-sama . . . That's the last name on the list we received.' Takarada-san, sitting on my right, handed me the final envelope. I compared it to the list, making sure there were no errors in the name or address.

'Great. No issues,' I said, handing the envelope to the woman sitting on my left. The envelopes already contained greetings and the restaurant announcement.

With a practised hand, the woman pasted down the flap and then sealed it with a stamp of a stylised version of a celebratory kanji. Then she flipped the envelope over and pasted a postal

Memo Pads

stamp for a happy occasion on the front. The whole process probably took less than ten seconds.

Before I could say anything, Takarada-san stood up and said, 'Thank you for coming.'

'No, thank you. It was so demanding of me to insist on confirming everything despite commissioning a pro . . . Not only was the handwriting beautiful, but there wasn't a single error. Nothing missing. It's wonderful. I truly admire your work.'

I meant that. At previous restaurants I'd worked at, we had sent out announcements when we opened a new branch, but in a hundred letters, there were always at least one or two mistakes. And on top of that, it was only natural that a few would be missing. That was why I had asked to inspect them, but my worries had been for nothing.

On the occasion of my setting up on my own, a broadcast script writer who believed in my abilities offered to produce the launch, and he introduced me to the venerable old stationery shop, Shihodo. I heard it was established in the year Tenpo 5. Tenpo 5 in the Western calendar is 1834, which, as I learned when I looked up the year, is not that long after Hanaya Yohei, who is said to have invented *nigiri sushi*, opened his restaurant in 1824.

I'd been nervous to see what sort of elderly person would be running the place, but I arrived to find an anticlimactically young manager. From the looks of him, I'd guess mid-thirties or so? Incidentally, his name is Ken Takarada – 'Ken written with the kanji for "inkstone",' he was kind enough to tell me.

At first I wasn't sure if I'd be able to count on him, but he handled all my requests with care, said clearly when something wasn't possible, and his price quotes and estimated delivery dates were as honest as they come. Apparently in the basement of this building that dated back to Showa 7 – 1932 – there's a letter press, but regarding the restaurant opening announcements, he vouched for someone else. 'I'm sorry, we can't do it in-house. But don't worry, I know a great artisanal printer.' He also arranged the copyist.

The woman who'd been sitting to my left stood and made a beautiful bow. 'Thank you so much for taking the time out of your busy launch schedule to personally inspect the mailings.' It was Kikuko Shirakawa-san, director of Tsukushikai and the one person who took on this job for me. Her rather short hair was completely white, which went well with her black collarless blouse. That, plus her black trousers and low-heeled pumps made her look less like the president of a copyist firm than a designer or painter. Apparently she also worked as a calligrapher and seal carver.

'It probably came off like I didn't trust you, so I'm sorry about that. Next time I won't require an inspection.' I stood and bowed to Shirakawa-san.

'Not at all! Really, I think there should be an inspection after each job. After all, a client will only use our services a few times in their life. Of course, we also check, but that's never an absolute guarantee, so I actually really appreciate you inspecting upon delivery,' Shirakawa-san replied with a smile. 'At any rate, thank you for your order. When I get back, I'll be sure to tell the staff who were involved in the project that Fuda-sama praised their work. I know they'll be delighted to hear it.'

Observing my conversation with Shirakawa-san, Takarada-san nodded emphatically. 'Tsukushikai's work is perfect every time. I always wonder how you keep from getting discouraged –

Memo Pads

with the expectations that everyone can perform, no mistakes...' Then he said, 'I'll make tea; please take a seat over there.'

The first floor of the shop, where this meeting took place, is often used for print-making or papercraft workshops, but that day he had offered the space to me. Actually the entire shop would normally be closed on this day, but he opened up especially for me, saying we could take our time going over the mailings.

It was a hardwood floor, and there were six worktables arranged in a rectangle in the centre. We'd made the inspection on one corner of that rectangle. Towards the windows on the right was a raised tatami area with a low table and three cushions set out.

'Ooh, *dorayaki* from Usagido!' Shirakawa-san's voice went up an octave. There was a gap between her sharp working demeanor and how cute she was once off duty. *I hope I can age so gracefully*, I thought.

'I happened to be nearby and was lucky enough to find they still had some,' Takarada-san said as he poured some water from the kettle into a tea bowl to cool.

Usagido is a sweet shop in Nihonbashi famous for its carefully selected ingredients and artisanal methods. While keeping to the traditions of formal confections used in tea ceremonies, they also prepare things like dorayaki and daifuku for casual snacks. Their subtle sweetness and soft texture make them popular. The dorayaki, especially, branded with an old-timey comic-style jumping rabbit on the pancakes, tend to sell out before noon. I've only gotten to eat one a handful of times.

'I actually went to elementary school and junior high with the present head of Usagido. But these are so popular that I hesitate

Letters from the Ginza Shihodo Stationery Shop

to ask him to hold some back for me just because we're friends, so I haven't had one in a long time.'

'Yeah, on the weekends, there's usually a queue outside before they even open. And the *amamidokoro* upstairs is always full. Or would you call it a "cafe" these days?'

Takarada-san nodded as he prepared the tea and handed it out along with the dorayaki set atop a piece of the paper used in tea ceremonies. 'They rebuilt their building around the time we were doing earthquake proofing, so it's been about five years. The previous shop only had three tables, but now on the first floor I think they have about thirty seats. In terms of business management, Usagido has got me beat.'

Once everyone had been served their tea and dorayaki, Shirakawa-san pressed her palms together and said, 'Itadakimasu!' I found myself echoing her.

When I took the cover off the tea bowl, the sweet scent of green tea wafted out. I sipped just enough to wet my mouth. The mellow fragrance immediately flowed clear through my nasal passages.

'Yum . . .' It slipped out before I realised.

Takarada-san emitted a sigh as if to say how relieved he was. 'I'm glad. As I was making it, I felt like it was a mistake. I mean, you're a top-class sushi chef, Fuda-sama. You serve tea and your sense of taste is so finely tuned. I regretted choosing green tea, thinking I could probably get away with coffee or black tea.'

'Ahh, but once you got ahold of such good dorayaki you knew that the only thing for it was green tea, huh?' said Shirakawa-san happily.

'Exactly!'

'I'm sorry you stressed out on my account. Actually, I'm not

Memo Pads

that well versed in tea. Of course, as someone who works in the food industry, I know my fair share, but . . . You know, at sushi restaurants we just pour hot water over the powdered sort, so we're not using such fine quality tea as you've served us.'

Shirakawa-san chomped into her dorayaki and murmured, 'Oh, right . . . I heard on TV or somewhere that tea made from the powder with hot water is great for washing down fish fat and the like. Is that true?'

I answered while eating my dorayaki. 'Yes, the water we pour of over the powder in the strainer is quite hot, which yields a tea that is lower in an umami element called theanine.'

'Theanine?' Shirakawa-san and Takarada-san's voices overlapped.

We all exchanged glances without really planning to. It was my first time meeting Shirakawa-san, and while I'd had several meetings with Takarada-san, it was only a few months prior that we'd met. Such a short time, and yet, how comfortable I felt with them. Working together, if only for a few hours, creates a connection. And they were both pros in their respective fields.

'Theanine is an amino acid that imparts a sweet, umami flavour. There's a lot of it in *gyokuro* and *sencha*.'

'I don't see anything wrong with umami . . . ?' Shirakawa-san, the first to finish her dorayaki, asked innocently.

'Right, you wouldn't think so, but actually the umami gets in the way. What a sushi restaurant is looking for in a tea is to remove any aftertaste. Of course, even gyokuro or sencha, with their high theanine content, can remove the taste and smell of fish, but in its place they leave a sweet umami. We don't want that.'

'Ohhh . . .'

They're both good listeners, I thought. From now on I'd be

Letters from the Ginza Shihodo Stationery Shop

alone before my cutting board. *I need to work on my listening skills*, I thought as I popped the last bite of dorayaki into my mouth. It really had an exquisite balance between pancake and bean paste. It had a strong flavour to enjoy while still being refreshing, and was satisfying and light at the same time.

'The tea is nice, but the dorayaki is wonderful. I can see why they're so popular. The flavours and textures of the cake, for instance, are the best of Japanese- and Western-style sweets – totally different from other dorayaki.'

Takarada-san nodded emphatically, teacup in hand. 'Apparently, they've adopted some Western ingredients and methods. As I mentioned earlier, I've been friends with the manager since childhood. The summer after our second year of high school, he abruptly declared he wouldn't be going to college and threw himself into studying languages – English, French, Italian. He'd decided that after graduating high school he would wander the world sampling all of its delicious foods. Like a culinary study abroad.'

'Wow, to decide something like that as a high schooler is pretty impressive,' Shirakawa-san marvelled. And I completely agreed with her. When I was a teen, I was just surviving day to day.

'Usagido used to do only traditional *wagashi*. So, of course sweets for tea ceremonies, but also *yokan*, *amanatto* and the like for sending as gifts, and these all sold well, but he said he didn't feel like the shop had a future that way. He decided, "I've eaten tasty foods all over the world and learned how to prepare them, so I'll transform Usagido into a confectionery the whole world can enjoy." And then he did exactly what he said he'd do. I think he's amazing.'

'And Usagido has two locations in Paris, one in New York

and one in London.' Takarada-san added that all of the branches were staffed by artisans who had trained at the main shop, and they never compromised on flavour, so they were doing well, especially with the exploding popularity of Japanese cuisine.

'Oh right, you spent some time overseas, too, didn't you, Fuda-sama? I read the magazine article.'

'I saw it, too. "A Novel Sushi Chef: Gin Fuda". You looked so cool in the photo. Though they didn't mention the details of where you trained.'

I nearly spat my tea out. *This is what they mean when they say 'breaking out in a cold sweat'.* The broadcast script writer producing my launch had been pitching to various media outlets, and it was true that a few magazines had featured me.

'Oh stop. It was nothing like the culinary study abroad your friend at Usagido did with his grand vision. It'd be more accurate to say I was drifting. So I can't talk specifics,' I said, shaking my head.

'Oh dear. Sorry to eat and run, but I need to get going,' said Shirakawa-san as she got to her feet after glancing at the clock.

'Thank you so much. I'm sure I'll make use of your services again. Let's keep in touch.' I moved the cushion out from under me, straightened up on the tatami, and bowed my head.

'None of that, please. It was an honour to do the job. Oh, Ken-chan, I'll take the envelopes.'

Having gone down onto the floor after Shirakawa-san, Takarada-san put the envelopes remaining on the worktable into a paper bag and handed it to her. It was a lot to mail, so Takarada-san told me it would be better to take them directly to the post office rather than using a postbox. Shirakawa-san said she would do it for me.

Letters from the Ginza Shihodo Stationery Shop

'Thanks, we'll take advantage of your kindness.' Takarada-san bowed to her.

'What are you saying? It's on my way back to the office! Anyhow, see you later.' With a 'Sorry to run!' she disappeared down the stairs. 'Stylish' was absolutely the word for her exit.

Having seen Shirakawa-san off, I took my Rhodia out of my pocket and glanced at my notes. Then I took out a pen and crossed off the last to-do with a single strike: *'opening announcement'*. But I left the parenthetical line below as it was.

'The Rhodia No. 12, right?'

Maybe it wasn't unusual for the manager of a venerable old stationery shop, but a glance at the cover was all he needed to identify the model of my memo pad.

'Yes, it's a good size for writing standing up, and the cover is waterproof, so I don't have to worry about handling it with wet hands. Plus it's easy to write on, and the pages are perforated in just the right way; ripping them off feels great.'

'We carry them, too. French and Italian chefs, as well as sommeliers, often buy them.'

'They are French memo pads, after all.'

I glanced down at my Rhodia and let out a small sigh. The parenthetical line I hadn't crossed out said, *'Send an announcement to Taisho, too.'*

'What's wrong?'

I hurriedly tried to regain composure, but when I looked at Takarada-san, I smiled sheepishly.

'Ah, it's just . . . I got the announcements finished, so almost everything is ready; I should be able to just focus on planning the menu and stocking the kitchen, but there's one thing I've left undone . . . and I'm not sure what to do about it."

Takarada-san nodded and waited in silence for me to continue. *Sometimes it really is better to avoid adding unnecessary comments*, I thought.

'I'm trying to decide if I should send an announcement to this one person or not...'

Takarada-san remained silent, using only his eyes to urge me to continue. I traced my pen around and around the line in parentheses.

'You know I'm a late bloomer, going independent at my age.'

Takarada-san shook his head. 'Fuda-sama, I don't think there's such a thing as too late in life. So please don't call yourself a late bloomer. That's a favour I'm asking of you.'

His kind words touched my heart. I nodded meekly. In exchange, I decided to ask him for something, too.

'Got it. Then I'd like to ask a favour of you as well.'

'Oh? What is it?' He seemed a bit surprised, and straightened his posture.

'Oh, no need to stand on ceremony. I just want to ask if you could stop using -sama. I can't get used to such formality... And "Fuda-sama" must be a pain to pronounce, too. Please use my personal name – Gin-san or Gin-chan. That's what everybody calls me, from customers to people at the market.'

Takarada-san exhaled deeply and cracked a relieved-seeming smile. 'Oh, good. I was worried it would be something more serious... Then I'll take the liberty of calling you Gin-san. I don't think I could manage "-chan" with a customer... Ah, there is one exception, but I've been calling him Sho-chan since before I was even in elementary school. Then Gin-san, please call me Ken-chan. Allow me to set that condition.'

'Got it, Ken-chan.'

Letters from the Ginza Shihodo Stationery Shop

'That's the spirit, Gin-san.'

We looked at each other and laughed.

'So what's the issue?'

I closed my Rhodia and stroked the orange cover with a finger.

'There's one person I didn't put on the list for the copyist, even though it's someone I'm truly indebted to.'

It's such a small thing, but simply calling each other Gin-san and Ken-chan seemed to shrink the distance between us. It felt much easier to talk to him.

'Hmm, that's sort of a surprise. I've only met you recently, and we've only talked briefly – and only about work – but I get the sense that you're sincere and conscientious. I don't get the sense that you'd neglect a benefactor. Who is it?'

I mentioned a *yoshoku* restaurant that's been around for ages in Asakusa.

'Oh, they're famous for their Hayashi rice, right? And their pork sauté and fried shrimp. I've been a few times.'

'Yeah, the dishes you mentioned are tasty of course, but the Hamburg steak, Naporitan and katsu sandwich are delicious, too. The crab cream croquettes and *menchikatsu* are also perfection.'

Ken-chan looked like he was about to start drooling. Though he always had a peaceful demeanour, he was such an efficient businessman that I had assumed he wasn't the type to enjoy small talk, but I guess I was wrong.

'You get hungry just thinking about it. Ahh, sipping cold bottled beer from a little glass while munching on fried shrimp with a drizzle of Worcestershire sauce would be the best. And after the beer, chilled sake. No putting on airs drinking wine. *Menchi* with plenty of *karashi* plus cups of room-temperature sake. Ahhh, what could be better?'

Memo Pads

This was also surprising to me. I figured that if he was the type to serve dorayaki he wouldn't be a drinker. Of course, some people with a sweet tooth swing both ways.

'But a yoshoku restaurant, huh? You're a sushi chef, so what's the connection?'

'Well, it'll be a long story if I get into it, but the one who provided me with the opportunity to get into the food and drink business is the *taisho* over there.'

'Oh, so you came up through yoshoku? There wasn't a single word in the magazine profile about that.'

'That makes sense – because I didn't talk about it.'

Ken-chan said, 'I'd like to hear about it if you don't mind.' I felt like talking to him might make me feel a bit better. Fiddling with my Rhodia in the palm of my hand, I began to tell my story.

Now I look pretty serious and call myself a sushi chef, but thirty years ago I was a so-called delinquent. There are plenty of people these days who say, "Back in the day I was a bit of a naughty boy," with an unconcerned look on their face, but I'm too embarrassed, so there's no way I could be so casual about it.

After graduating junior high, I started at the local high school, but I didn't even make it halfway through the year before dropping out. Relying on contacts to make it to Tokyo was all well and good, but there wasn't any work for an unskilled delinquent to do. Even in the rare instances I found a job, it wouldn't last long; I didn't have a stable situation.

It seems strange to me now, but I have almost no memories of that time. For the first year or so I crashed with friends or older acquaintances, or at the houses of people I met out and about. I was a one-outfit wonder with no luggage besides a daypack.

Letters from the Ginza Shihodo Stationery Shop

It was the taisho who took me in. I was seventeen, and he must have been in his mid-forties. I went over the hill years ago, but I still can't believe I'm older now than he was then.

I met him in Ueno. I didn't have anywhere to stay, so I'd sleep on park benches. It was the hottest part of the summer, and the sun was brutal, so I'd been shifting benches since morning to chase the shade. During one of those shifts, I happened to find a ticket to the Tokyo National Museum. It had probably been blown out of the hand of a guide or a tour conductor with a group of people.

At first I thought, *Tch! Wish it were cash! Or at least a movie ticket.* But as the sun rose higher in the sky, the temperature soared, and I realised, *They might have air conditioning in the museum!*

I'd never had any interest in the Tokyo National Museum, so I had no idea what kind of place it was. Looking from outside the fence, my only thought was, *What a fancy building that is.* But when I entered, I was surprised. I stood up straighter without thinking, or like, the atmosphere could trick me into feeling smarter, more refined. There was something about the air.

I still go a few times a year, and I always feel like it resets me. I'm not entirely sure why. Going through the gate and surveying the grounds, walking into the main building and looking up at the grand staircase – I get this feeling that's so hard to describe. I think it must be because it takes me back to the way I was when I first met the taisho.

I remember it vividly, even now: the taisho was absorbed by a rubbing of *Ranteijo*. At the time, I hadn't heard of *Ranteijo*, much less Wang Xizhi, and I had no idea what a rubbing was. All I thought was, *There's an older guy looking really hard at that black paper covered in white characters.*

Memo Pads

After noticing him, I went around to look at some other things, but when I returned, he was still examining the piece. I figured it must be something really great, so I stopped to take a proper look. Even I, with my lack of education, could read some parts of it. Not that it made any sense to me, of course. But I did find the characters themselves pretty.

Then, out of nowhere, the man spoke to me.

'Do you like it?' He looked me up and down real quick. His face in profile was handsome. He was stylish in a dogtooth suit with a white shirt and a black knit tie.

He had asked me a question, so I felt like I needed to answer, but I couldn't think of anything clever to say. In the end, I just said exactly what I thought.

'I think the characters are pretty.'

'Yeah, wish I could write this nicely . . .' said the taisho, staring at the piece again. We stood there next to each other for a good five minutes studying the *Ranteijo*.

Then he suddenly said, 'There's something else really nice over there.'

He set off without waiting for me to reply. I followed him to find a flat display cabinet.

'It's a *tekagami*.'

'A tekagami?'

He nodded and explained. 'The "te" here – the hand – means handwriting, i.e., the characters. And the "kagami" part is the same character as the second one in *zukan* – an illustrated encyclopedia, and it means "precedent" or "model". In other words, a tekagami is a collection of reference calligraphy.'

'Reference calligraphy?'

'*Ranteijo*, the rubbing we were looking at before, was taken from a stone monument that had a copy of writing said to be by Wang Xizhi. Well, it's basically the original tekagami. People long ago would collect old samples like these and study calligraphy by following the examples.'

'Hmm.'

I wasn't sure how to react to being told that this was how they had studied because every last bit of this was new to me. He spent another thirty minutes or so looking at that display cabinet. Partway through, he took a memo pad with an orange cover out of his pocket and jotted something down with a pen.

'What are you writing?'

'Oh this? I'm copying a bit of the description here. I want to look it up at the library next time I go.'

'. . . I see.'

I'd never met an adult like this before, so I was truly surprised. No one around me had ever taken notes.

'I'm a dummy, so if I don't write things down, I'll forget them right away. But mysteriously, if I write them down, I don't forget. Why is that, huh?'

Don't ask me, I thought.

After such a long interaction I couldn't just say, 'Well, bye then,' so I stayed there looking at it with him. Then he suddenly said, 'It's lunchtime. Let's go grab a bite.'

'I'm OK,' I replied quickly. I don't think I had even one hundred yen on me.

'Naw, c'mon,' he said, and set off. I had no choice but to follow him.

We left the museum and walked for about ten minutes to a restaurant.

The taisho seemed to have come any number of times and

Memo Pads

followed the staff in an accustomed way to the seats they offered us. I followed hesitantly.

Tables covered with white cloths sat on the hardwood floor, and at each seat was an ornamental dish with a fancily folded napkin on top. *I'm really glad I was able to take a bath and wash my clothes at the last place I stayed.* The restaurant was so clean and bright that thoughts like this crossed my mind.

'Is there anything you'd like to eat?' the taisho asked me while he browsed the menu. I'd been given a menu as well, but one look at the prices had me worried.

'No, nothing in particular.'

'Then I'll order for the both of us.'

He called the server over and ordered salad, an assortment of fried foods, shrimp gratin and Hamburg steak.

'Also, a beer for me and a large order of rice for him,' he added at the end.

Enthusiastically drinking his beer once it had come out, he told me, 'I've never met the owner of this restaurant, but I think they must be quite a talent. They use quality ingredients unsparingly, preparing them so carefully, yet also price everything so conscientiously.'

All the food that came out had a polished presentation and tasted great. Taisho murmured things like, 'Aha', and, 'Oh, this is good', as he ate, sometimes taking out his memo pad to write something down.

'Um, what are you aha-ing about?' I asked, shamelessly, partly because I'd let my guard down with a full belly. These days, there's no way I could ask something like that.

'Hm? Oh, I'm a cook. I run a yoshoku restaurant in Asakusa. So eating out counts as research for me. The reason I said

Letters from the Ginza Shihodo Stationery Shop

"Aha" before was . . . you saw those bow-shaped noodles, right? Those are called farfalle, but anyhow, they came out dressed in balsamic vinegar and pepper as a side to the fried stuff. Most places just give you shredded cabbage and tomato. Well, and maybe a slice of lemon to add some colour. But here they add julienned cucumber to the salad for a deeper green, and instead of tomato, they use decoratively cut radishes. And lots of places throw out some spaghetti sauteed in ketchup, but here they got a little creative with the farfalle. That's why that impressed "aha" slipped out.'

'. . . I see.'

'You can tell the person running the kitchen here pays attention to detail. They also make sure that the sides don't overpower the fried items themselves. The French fries that came with the Hamburg steak were also freshly fried, and the buttered peas, carrots and corn were carefully selected and prepared just so despite the hassle. Well worthy of respect.'

I suddenly felt embarrassed for chowing down without any other impressions besides *Yum!*

'Part of the reason I come to the museum is to stop by this restaurant.'

'Even though you run a yoshoku restaurant, you look forward to coming to the same kind of place?'

The taisho nodded emphatically. 'Yeah, no matter what I eat, wherever I go, I learn something new. That goes for Western, Japanese or Chinese cuisine. I eat fast food, and I buy hot bento at those chain shops. They all use creativity within their various constraints to deliver something tasty and nutritious, you know?'

He was confident in his own cooking, but he would never disparage another restaurant. Even if he saw or heard something

Memo Pads

that didn't impress him, he remained silent. If anything, he might say, 'Let's make sure we don't do it that way at our place.'

After we finished our food, he ordered us coffee. He didn't smoke during or after our meal. Unlike today, back then most places allowed smoking, and there were a lot of adults smoking around us.

'You don't smoke?'

He frowned sharply and shook his head. 'No, I don't. Cooking keeps you on your feet and it's pretty hard work, so lots of people like to smoke, but I'm not a fan. It's the smell that gets me. Even if you wash your hands, it sticks to your fingers – and your hair, and your clothes. It could ruin the food I put so much effort into making. Do you smoke?'

'If I have the money . . . Or if someone gives me a fag.'

'If that's the extent of your habit, you should quit while you can. We know it's bad for our health, and the cost adds up. Once you're addicted, then there's no helping it, but if you can live without them when you can't afford it, then you're better off quitting now.'

'Yeah, I guess so.'

I didn't feel at all like I was being lectured. Our age gap was wide enough for us to be father and son, but our conversation felt to me more like being persuaded by an older brother. I think that's why I was able to listen.

'By the way, what kind of work are you in? If you're at the museum on a weekday, it can't be a nine-to-five job. And you're so young – you could be in school. Oh, but first, tell me your name.'

It was strange, he treated this kid to lunch and taught him all sorts of things without even knowing his name. That's the kind of guy he is, though.

Letters from the Ginza Shihodo Stationery Shop

I told him how I'd come to Tokyo from the countryside, how I didn't have a stable job, how I was just surviving day to day. People I met out and about sometimes asked my origins, but I never really gave a proper answer. I was embarrassed that I didn't have my act together.

But I told the taisho everything, including the fact that I was both unemployed and homeless. It made me nervous, but I felt like lying to him would be a mistake.

'I see . . .' he murmured, before folding his arms and staring at his coffee cup in silence for a few moments. I don't remember how long it was. I think it must have been a few seconds, or a minute at most, but it felt like a really long time.

'Then why don't you come work for me? A guy just quit.'

'Huh?'

I was shocked by this invitation that came out of nowhere. At most I figured he might say he could introduce me to an acquaintance looking for a part-time worker.

'A-ah, but I don't have any cooking experience. I've never even held a knife. I'd only get in your way.'

He unfolded his arms and gave me a little smile. 'If you could get in my way, that'd be something! Well, at first, you'll have no idea what's what, so the most you'll be able to do is stand there staring. But don't worry. No one can do anything in the beginning. Everyone working at my restaurant started as an amateur, including me. A few graduated from culinary school, but even those guys are useless in the beginning. So you don't have to worry about the skill side.'

'. . . Oh.'

He continued to talk as he signalled the server for our bill. 'I can teach you all the techniques. The rest is up to you.

Memo Pads

No matter how skilled a person is, if they're rotten inside, they can't make good food. Conversely, if you're green, but your heart's in the right place and you have the drive to improve, you'll be fine.'

The taisho looked over the bill, grabbed a long wallet out of his inner jacket pocket, and took out a brand-new 10,000-yen note. He slipped it under the binder clip the bill was sandwiched beneath and handed it back to the server. 'It's not much, but keep the change as a tip.' Then he stood and clapped me on the shoulder. 'All right, let's go. Today we're closed, so there's no one at the restaurant, but there might be someone at the apartment dorms.'

'The taisho seems like a cool guy,' Ken-chan said, after listening quietly.

'Yeah, he really was. He has a great sense of aesthetics, I guess you could say, or rather, he's so refined . . . no matter what he did, he did it with style. And he carried himself so well, too. At his restaurant, the kitchen and the floor are strictly separated, and customers never see the cooks at work, but he always stood as straight as a rod. The way he handled the pots and frying pans always seemed like a dance.'

'I think this must have been a long time ago, but I don't think there were many people who paid tips back then. And to do it so casually – that's hard to imitate.'

It's not that no one in Japan adds a gratuity to their bill, but as Ken-chan observed, they're in the minority. There are many places that automatically take a percentage of the cheque as a service charge, and customers probably aren't eager to tip on top of that.

Letters from the Ginza Shihodo Stationery Shop

'He only ever kept new bills in his wallet. He'd say it felt better to pay with neat, clean money. Oh right, you give change in new bills and coins at Shihodo, too, don't you? Maybe you two have something in common.'

Ken-chan smiled before nodding. 'The customers are always surprised and delighted, and I enjoy seeing their reactions. So what happened next?'

The taisho took me to an apartment building not far from his restaurant. The room in the back on the ground floor was his, and his employees stayed in the other five rooms. Apparently, the landlord was a regular at the restaurant and rented the building out to him for a song. Taisho paid the rent for all six rooms in a lump sum and didn't charge employees anything to live there.

The three rooms on the first floor were full of people who had been working there for a while, but there were two free rooms on the ground floor. In the end, I decided to take the one closest to the entrance. My only belongings were the change of clothes and toothbrush in my daypack, so there was nothing to 'move in'.

'I'll get you a futon tomorrow, so for tonight, sleep on this,' said the taisho taking a sleeping bag out of the closet.

'Uh, this is fine. A futon would be wasted on me.'

'Hm? Are you trying to be polite or something?'

'Err, no, it's just . . .'

He grinned. 'It feels like you're declaring your intent to skedaddle. Well, do whatever makes you happy. I think it'll be cold in the winter, but you'll probably be fine for a while.'

That night when the other employees got back from enjoying

their day off, he said he was throwing a welcome party in his room to introduce me. He must have ducked out to shop at some point, because there was *sukiyaki* ready.

'This is Gin Fuda. Everyone be nice to him. Hmm, is going by Gin OK with you? Fuda is kind of a hard name to call someone.'

With that word from the taisho, everyone decided on calling me Gin. All three of them were from the countryside too, and the eldest was only three years older than me. The other two were just a year older than I was, and had been working for the restaurant less than a year. They were all good guys, and I was never teased or bullied. And of course, the taisho always kept an eye out to make sure of that.

After clearing up after dinner that night, the five of us went to the neighbourhood bathhouse. Nowadays even the smallest studio apartment will have a shower, but back then it was more common for a wooden apartment building not to have baths.

The taisho announced to the woman staffing the entrance, 'This is our new guy, Gin,' and then we went in without paying. I found out later that he paid the bill for the five of us at the end of each month.

He had tabs like this all over the neighbourhood – naturally at places that sold vegetables, meat, fish and condiments, but also at the pharmacy and a hardware shop, a stationery shop and even a barber. We could just say, 'Put it on Taisho's tab, please.' In other words, I could survive without a single yen. I appreciated it so much because I had nothing. In exchange, however, when I went for a haircut, the only option was a buzz. The taisho's policy was that we could worry about looking sexy after we learned how to do our jobs, and while we lived in the dorm, we weren't allowed to choose our own haircuts. But as a result, it was hard to feel like messing around. I couldn't very well go to a disco or a club with a shaved head.

In the kitchen, aside from the three guys I'd met were two cooks who commuted. They, along with the taisho, did all the cooking. The oldest of the live-ins was like an apprentice cook, and the other two mainly did prep work and were desperate to help out even a little with the actual cooking. Of course, as the newbie, I was in charge of dishwashing. Day in and day out, I washed plates, glasses, pots and pans.

Even so, I was given a pristine white cook's hat and coat. I wore a large rubber-coated apron over the top, and fought my battles at the washing station. At first I washed in the way I was taught by the other guys, but bit by bit I got the hang of it and came up with my own little tricks. I experimented with soaps, brushes and sponges, and it was so interesting; every time I tried something new, I found there was more to discover.

For pots and frying pans, it's important to get the grease off while they're still hot, whereas for plates, if I scraped any food waste and sauce off with a spatula and soaked them in lukewarm water with some neutral detergent, the dirty bits would float to the surface, and a wipe with a sponge would be enough to get them clean. Scrubbing dishes too hard can scratch the glass or damage any design, so the key is to see how much gunk you can get to float off and how quickly you can clean them.

I was also happy to discover that the way you dry dishes makes a big difference. In a restaurant, you have to wipe a ton of dishes dry, so the amount of time you can spend on each one is limited. But if you wipe them clumsily, they won't shine despite being freshly washed. I tried different grips on the cloth and

Memo Pads

different wiping orders and figured out a method for leaving no wet spots in a short amount of time.

Thanks in part to those efforts, the time I spent washing dishes gradually decreased. Although none of it was that big of a deal, seeing results after thinking for myself – like lunchtime dishes being done thirty minutes faster or closing cleanup taking fifteen fewer minutes – made me happy.

And Taisho noticed, too.

He would find moments to give me attention, like, 'Oh, the dishes are looking nicer than before!' or, 'You've really got the hang of keeping the washing station neat.' That made me happy, too. It was like I'd received his approval.

Before too long, he said, 'Hey, Gin, if you've got some time on your hands, why don't you come and help me?' and I was allowed to set foot in the circle beyond the washing station.

Of course, at first I was doing essentially prep for the prep – jobs like washing the dirt off the vegetables we got directly from farmers and shredding salad leaves by hand – but the thought that the veg I'd washed would be used in the food was a thrill. In hindsight, I can see that I was so pure back then. I was so happy to do any task I was being allowed to do for the first time.

In the winter, obviously, the water was cold. For the dishes, I could use the gas-powered heater, but I had to wash the vegetables in the frigid water, which was pretty miserable. I had no time to complain, though. If I didn't get them washed up promptly, I'd make problems for the whole kitchen. By that time, I was capable of keeping such things in mind.

Of course, rubber gloves would have been an option, but then you can't feel anything. Things you might miss with your eyes are easy to spot through touch. This remains true today; I can

Letters from the Ginza Shihodo Stationery Shop

tell if an ingredient is no good just by setting it on the palm of my hand. So I learned from washing vegetables that no matter how cold it is, you have to touch things directly with your hands.

Around the time I'd been working at the taisho's restaurant for about a year, he said to me, on a day before our day off, 'Gin, I want you to come with me somewhere tomorrow.'

The next day we went to Kappabashi. He took me to a knife shop and showed me the chef's knives.

'Try holding a few of them,' he said. And I got to wrap my fingers around some knife handles.

'I think maybe this one . . . The heft, the grip. It feels like it's attracted to my hand.'

Taisho nodded deeply.

'This one, please. And please choose a whetstone for it as well.'

When I tried to take everything once it was wrapped, he said, 'It's fine, I'll carry it,' and I couldn't get him to let go of it.

Then he said, 'Let's have coffee before we head home,' and we went into a cafe. After ordering, he looked at me with the most serious face I've ever seen him make and said, 'Hey, do you have five yen?'

I must have looked puzzled by the abruptness of the question.

'When you put a dubious expression on that stupid-looking face of yours, your ugliness stands out even more. You must have five yen, right? Hurry up, get it out.'

'Yeah, I think . . .'

I took a five-yen coin out of the coin purse in my pocket.

'OK, I'll sell this to you for five yen.'

He offered me the paper bag in his lap.

'Huh?'

'Just give me the five yen. And take the bag.'

Memo Pads

I had no idea what was going on, but I had no choice but to do as he said.

'Sold!'

'Thank you.'

'No, you're supposed to say, "Bought!"'

'... Bought.'

And finally the sale was made. But with the whetstone and everything, it had ended up being quite a sum, so I had no idea what the point of trading it for a single five-yen coin was.

'OK, now that's yours. Use it well and take good care of it. The more love you show a tool, the more reliable it will be.'

'... Thank you. But why did we have to go through the "Sold! Bought!" thing?'

The taisho heaved an exaggerated sigh and rolled his eyes. 'Listen, you've got a lot more studying to do. Oh, hang on, I meant to give this to you, too.'

He took a memo pad with an orange cover and a pen out of his pocket.

'From now on, I want you to carry this pad when you're at work, obviously, but also on your day off. Write down things that catch your attention and things people caution you about – all of them. Any kind of memo pad is fine, but I use the Rhodia No. 12. It's the perfect size to hold in the palm of your hand and scribble in, and the cover is waterproof so you can handle it with wet hands, no problem.'

I accepted the Rhodia and pen.

'Studying doesn't just mean reading, writing and arithmetic like you learn at school. If you don't know things, you'll be constantly racking up losses. You won't notice when a chance is passing you by and you won't see where there's a trap. Well, this

Letters from the Ginza Shihodo Stationery Shop

can't be forced if you don't want to take it to heart, so I won't harp on about it, but... At any rate, take notes on what you don't know or don't understand, things you're hearing for the first time – any and everything.'

'OK...'

'Anyhow, getting back on topic, you must never give a person a blade as a present – it would mean you're "cutting ties" with them. This applies not only to chef's knives, but scissors and so on too. Combs are also no good – that's because *kushi* sounds the same as the word for "painful death".'

'Wow, I never knew that.'

I immediately opened my Rhodia and wrote, 'Never give blades or combs as gifts.'

The taisho seemed satisfied to see that, and he continued. 'Blades and combs have various interpretations, actually. Some people say blades are appropriate gifts because they "carve a path to the future" and some people insist that the meaning of a comb is "disentangling". But yeah, I think if we sense even a shadow of bad luck, we shouldn't risk it. So with a knife, it's better to be safe and make a sale.'

'Oh, thank you. But I feel bad that you sold me such an expensive knife for just five yen.'

Taisho burst out laughing and said, 'It's a reward for working so hard over the past year! I just had to be there with you when you chose your first knife. The guy who runs that shop is too honest for his own good, so he sells nice stuff at reasonable prices. If you ever want more knives, you should talk to him. He remembers his customers and will find whatever it is you need.'

Then, on our way home, he introduced me to all sorts of other shops. 'This place is good for pots,' he told me, and, 'For frying pans, this place is best.' I noted down the names of the shops. It had taken no time to fill in ten pages of my new memo pad.

'Keep taking notes like that! You can buy those pads at Tamatamaya.'"

Tamatamaya was the stationery shop he had a tab at.

Starting the next day, I was allowed to help with prep work, so day in, day out, most of my battles were fought with vegetables – peeling, chopping and so on. Incidentally, at Taisho's restaurant, for things like pots, cutting boards and ladles and whatnot we used the restaurant's equipment, but each cook brought their own preferred knives and frying pans. Obviously Taisho had a number of knives, but so did the other two cooks, which they carried to and from the restaurant in special lockable cases. They all handled their knives with care, never failing to sharpen them after a day's work.

Seeing that attitude, naturally, we trainees learned to take good care of our knives. Taisho was single, and after work, he'd invite the live-in guys over to teach us every step of maintaining different kitchen equipment. Of course I took down every word he said in my Rhodia. Most of the things I learned back then, the skills I gained, still support me as a cook today.

In the year after I started using them, I filled up over thirty Rhodias with notes.

'That's kind of a great story. I remember hearing a famous chef on TV say something like, "An owner-chef has to be both a cook and a manager. Management means getting the most out of your people – that is, your ability to develop your personnel will determine the success of your business,"' Ken-chan said, nodding.

Letters from the Ginza Shihodo Stationery Shop

'When I decided to open my own place, I thought about hiring people, but I decided not to. The reason I decided to start with an eight-seat counter that doesn't serve lunch, and in fact serves only eight meals at dinner, is that I can do it without staff. In that sense, with six in the kitchen and four on the floor – ten people in total – Taisho was really amazing. Now that I'm opening my own restaurant, small though it may be, it really hits me just how amazing he was.'

'Yeah . . . I'm managing to run this place because I can do it at my own pace by myself. If you asked me to run a stationery shop with staff, I'm not sure I could.'

I nodded deeply as I continued.

Three years passed, so it was my fourth summer at Taisho's restaurant.

Of the three guys ahead of me, two quit, and one got married and left the dorm. Before I'd realised, three guys had joined the team after me, but they all commuted from home, so Taisho and I were the only ones left in the dorm.

Partly because it was so fun, I learned more and more about what it meant to be a cook fairly quickly. My Rhodia really came in so handy at work. By then, I'd developed the habit of rewriting and organising my notes from the memo pads in a big notebook before bed. Only a handful of years prior I'd been just surviving day to day, but through meeting the taisho, everything had changed.

As those fulfilling days accumulated, I was eventually entrusted with making the soup stock and seasoning the vegetable sides. My goal was to keep training so that someday I'd be able to work the frying pan like Taisho.

Memo Pads

But that wasn't to be.

When I first arrived in Tokyo, someone I met in Shinjuku helped me out for a while. I found out later that he was part of a loose gang raking in cash by, essentially, committing crime. I never helped directly with his jobs, but I did watch his office while he was out in exchange for pocket money. No, I suppose it was too much to call it pocket money. I think it was basically hush money.

In the end, the cops caught him. With nowhere else to go, I drifted to Ueno. At first I felt like I was really in trouble, but actually I think if I had stayed in Shinjuku, I would have ended up getting involved in some kind of scheme.

That guy finished serving his prison sentence and got out. And he happened across a feature on Taisho's restaurant in a magazine and spotted me in the photo of the staff outside.

I opened the back door to take the trash out one night, and he was standing there.

'Long time no see. Take a look at you! Is that a cook's coat or whatever they call it? It suits you.' Standing under the streetlight with a creepy grin, he went on. 'When you're done in there, come and meet me.' He handed me a box of matches from a little bar in the neighbourhood.

When business ended for the day, I raced through cleanup and hurried over to the bar. It was a typical hole in the wall, and no other customers were there.

'Do you enjoy your job?'

I just nodded silently.

'I think I'm going to start working again, too. How about it? Will you help me out?'

All I had to do was sit in an office and answer a phone

Letters from the Ginza Shihodo Stationery Shop

and I would make multiple times the monthly salary I got at the taisho's place. My old self would have surely jumped at the chance.

'Sorry, I have no intention of leaving my current job.'

When I moved to stand up, he parried with, 'Well, hang on,' and looked me in the eye. 'When the cops picked me up, I didn't give them your name. "I was only answering the phone in the office", doesn't really fly as an excuse. Then, as now, I thought I could trust you.'

'Don't make things up. I may have flopped around the office, but I never helped with your work.'

'You took the compensation, didn't you?'

I was speechless. He'd said it was an allowance, but now he was calling it compensation.

'Y-you said to think of it as an allowance!'

He lit a cigarette and took a slow drag.

'In prison, alcohol and tobacco are forbidden by law. Of course, there are loopholes, and sometimes I managed to have a fag. Though I could never take my time like this. It was like being a middle schooler trying to sneak in a smoke when the teacher isn't looking. Talk about miserable. Actually, did you quit smoking?'

'I did. Smoking doesn't benefit a cook in any way.'

Looking offended, he stubbed out his cigarette and downed the rest of his drink.

'OK, got it. I won't force you, but I do have one condition.'

'... What's the condition?'

'The money I gave you – I want it back. I was thriving back then, so I think I gave you two or three *zuku* at a time. A conservative estimate couldn't be less than three million, right?'

Memo Pads

'Zuku' is a gambling term for a bundle of ten 10,000-yen notes. And it was true that each time he paid me it'd be at least 100,000, and occasionally up to 500,000.

'I don't have that kind of money.'

He shook his head. 'You've got a job, haven't you? I'm not saying you have to pay it all at once. Just give me a million for starters. And the other two million can come in instalments of 500,000 over five months.'

'... Three million suddenly became three and a half million.'

He shook his head back and forth in amusement. 'Wow, so you can do maths in your head now. Back when you were working for me, you couldn't even remember a phone number.'

I stood up without saying anything.

'Come here tomorrow with a million yen. As you can see, I know where you work, but I've also got your address. And if you mess this up I'll show up at the restaurant.'

Then he took a card case out of his breast pocket and handed me one of his cards.

'I quit the small-time shit, too. I met someone worth calling *family*.'

On the card was the crest of an instantly recognisable *yakuza* clan. These days anyone flashing around a card like that would fall immediately foul of the Act on Prevention of Unjust Acts by Organised Crime Group Members, but back then things were still lax.

I have no recollection of how I got back to my room after that. When I reached the apartment building, I ran into Taisho on his way back from the bathhouse.

'Hey, where've you been? The bath's gonna close if you don't hurry up.'

Letters from the Ginza Shihodo Stationery Shop

When I saw Taisho's cheerful expression by the light of the moon, I thought, *I can't cause trouble for him.*

Ken-chan must have been listening with bated breath, because he suddenly exhaled deeply.

'Things developed so quickly I'm getting tired just listening.'

I nodded. 'Yeah. Well, in the end, I packed up my stuff and left Tokyo that night – only the important stuff: minimal clothing, cash and my bankbook, plus the knife from Taisho, my Rhodia, and my notebooks. I ripped a page out of the Rhodia, wrote, "I realise this is sudden, but I'm taking the liberty of quitting", and slipped it into Taisho's postbox along with the key to my room. Then I went straight to the long-haul bus leaving from the Yaesu exit of Tokyo Station and fled to Kansai.'

'So abrupt . . .' Ken-chan said sadly.

'Yeah, I felt like it was what I got for leaving things in my past so unresolved. I headed to Tokyo, went with the flow, took money I knew was no good, and used it on pointless stuff. I knew I'd been an idiot, but there wasn't anything I could do about it.'

'Why didn't you talk to the taisho? You were a minor when you connected with that shady guy, weren't you? Plus, he was just spouting off his mouth. If you had taken it to the police, they might have been able to help.'

It was exactly as Ken-chan said.

'Yeah. But I didn't know anything back then, so I was convinced that if I stuck around, I would cause trouble for the taisho. I was so stupid, just like he said. I didn't study, so I didn't know anything. I didn't understand. I let the threat frighten me and ran away. That's what a small, wretched person I was.'

Memo Pads

Ken-chan shook his head vigorously. 'I'm sure that's not true. I don't think you'd be the you you are today if that were the case.'

'Hmm, maybe not. I hope you're right. Well, I found work almost immediately upon arriving in Kansai. I dipped into my savings to find somewhere I could settle, but I sent the rest by registered post to the yakuza. Of course, it wasn't a million yen, but I gave him as much as I had. And after that, every time I got paid, I sent most of it to him. So, it took a year and a half, but I managed to pay off the amount he'd quoted to me.'

'Wow. And he didn't come after you? To Kansai?'

I shook my head. Honestly, I'd been worrying about when he would show up again. But he never did. Maybe he figured since I was sending him money, it wasn't worth the transportation costs to go out of his way to threaten me.

'What's that unforgiving guy doing now, I wonder.'

'He died. Got caught up in some kind of feud. Almost at the exact same time I finished paying him off. I remember it vividly. I was at a Chinese restaurant eating *gyoza* and fried rice when I happened to see the news on TV.'

'Wow. I realise this isn't exactly a tactful thing to say, but if he was going to die, it's too bad he couldn't have done it sooner. Then you wouldn't have had to work so hard paying off such a meaningless debt.'

'No, I'm glad he lived till I'd paid him off. It allowed me to feel like I'd settled things. But it was so anticlimactic. I really didn't want to be in Japan anymore.'

Ken-chan pounded his palm as if to say he'd made the connection. 'So that's why you went on your drifting travels, huh?'

'... Basically, yes.'

His sunny expression suddenly darkened. 'But if that's what

Letters from the Ginza Shihodo Stationery Shop

happened, then you should definitely send an opening announcement to your taisho.'

'Well, yeah. That's why it's on my mind.'

Ken-chan began to clear the table, putting my tea bowl on a tray. 'Umm, this is a request from me. Please send him an announcement. I'll prepare the stationery. Wait just a moment.' The calm atmosphere we'd had vanished all at once. With that resolute declaration, he left the room, tray in hand.

Sheesh, did I get carried away and say too much? I sort of regretted it.

When I glanced outside, I saw a mackerel sky. Through the open window came the kind of pleasant, somewhat wet, wind that blows only in the autumn.

'Sorry for the wait.'

Ken-chan must have come jogging up the stairs from the sales floor below. He was panting a little as he handed me some stuff.

'I think this paper and envelope will be good. It's elegant and suitable for general use. And then, to write, use this pen. I chose one that has a smooth action. Since I selected everything at my discretion, I won't charge you. Please write to the taisho and tell him everything that happened and that you're opening a restaurant. Oh, and we can put the announcement envelope and the letter together in a larger envelope to mail them. I'll arrange everything.'

Ken-chan had made a complete return to his role as the manager of Shihodo.

'Thanks, but . . . I've never written a letter in my life.'

My voice hardly sounded like me; it was so feeble, and I felt pathetic.

Ken-chan thrust the stationery and pen into my hands, said,

Memo Pads

'Come on, let's do this!' and had me put my shoes on. Then he ushered me into the chair before the big, old desk on the opposite side of the room.

'I'll leave you alone for a bit. Please take your time writing. I'll bring up some fresh tea later.'

With that, he went down the stairs.

Left on my own, I was forced to confront the blank white paper. I thought maybe I should write a traditional seasonal greeting, but decided in the end to leave it out and just start with, 'It's been a long time.'

First, I wrote a frank apology for going into hiding without saying anything. And I explained why: that a yakuza I knew before I met him had come after me to collect a debt, so I was forced to run away.

I explained how, thinking back now, I regretted not consulting with him directly. How I fled to Kansai and frantically worked multiple jobs – a cafe, an *udon* shop and others – in order to pay back the entire amount.

How I felt so aimless after paying off the debt, that I went to Europe with no real plan. How I travelled around by working to save up the money to move again. How everywhere I went, I got a job at a restaurant, always starting with washing dishes and doing prep work, but that thanks to his training, from his place, I always earned respect in no time. How I went here and there, learning the fundamentals of French, Italian and German cuisine. How I used a hundred Rhodia No. 12s during that time and copied my notes into ten notebooks.

How after Europe, I went to the United States and a restaurant owner I met at a supermarket that stocked Japanese

Letters from the Ginza Shihodo Stationery Shop

ingredients aggressively recruited me, saying, 'You're Japanese, you must be able to make Japanese food.' How I made sushi, tempura, sukiyaki and pretty much everything else, but developed a complex about the fact that I'd never learned the fundamentals and came back to Japan because I wanted to start over from the beginning.

How it took ten years from leaving his restaurant for me to return to Japan. How I'd retrained from scratch at a sushi restaurant and was finally opening my own place.

How I'd continued to use Rhodia memo pads since returning, too, and how I had ten cardboard boxes full of notes . . .

All the episodes felt like they were going to overflow out of my head at once, so I hemmed and hawed over what to write, and my pen dragged. I had never once imagined making a living as a chef, so if it weren't for the taisho taking me in and patiently teaching me, I wouldn't be who I am. The more that thought sank in, the more my hand shook, and I couldn't keep writing.

Confronting my life so far by writing it down like this, it became clear that Taisho taught me more than just cooking; he taught me how to take notes, how to study and how a person should live. I'm sure the reason I was accepted in Kansai, in Europe, in the United States, and then at the sushi restaurant when I knocked on their door upon returning to Japan, was that Taisho trained me in the fundamentals of being human.

'Your knife, chopping board, pots and so on are tools of your trade. Take as good care of them as if they were your hands and arms. If you don't, they won't do what you want them to.

'Anyone who is wasteful with ingredients won't improve. Vegetables, beef, pork, fish – they were all once living things. Humans have forced them to yield to our convenience. That is, we

Memo Pads

rob them of their lives. We need to show our gratitude by not wasting anything. And the producers – farmers, fishers, ranchers – are all working so hard. If we're truly thankful for their labour, then we can't be careless with the fruits of it.'

These lessons had been repeated to me over and over, decades ago, but I could still remember them clearly.

'Get a haircut every three weeks, at least. It's a buzz, so even if you throw in a shave it'll only take about thirty minutes, right? Also, take a bath even if you're feeling a little under the weather. Poor health is usually just proof that you're not taking care of yourself. Cut your nails every three days. And in the morning when you wash your face, check your nose to make sure there are no hairs poking out. Cleanliness is the most basic requirement for a cook. Always button up your cook's coat and wear your hat straight. Wash the coat if you've worn it even once. And then iron it. Some people pay close attention to things like that.'

Actually, I seem to remember him finding a cheap iron at a pawnshop and buying it for me.

'Whenever you say, "Good morning", "Hello", "Thank you", or, "I'm sorry", make sure it's loud and clear. If the person you're talking to doesn't hear you, it's the same as if you never said it at all.

'Invest half of your salary in yourself. Do you understand what I mean by "invest"? First, buy yourself good tools. If you care for quality equipment, it will last you your whole life. You should also try eating at first-rate restaurants. It'll help train your eye and you can learn from how other chefs innovate.

'Visit art and history museums, see movies and plays, read books – push yourself to acquire culture. The people who say, "I don't get it", or, "It's boring" just haven't really given whatever it is a chance.

Letters from the Ginza Shihodo Stationery Shop

'If you visit an art museum a hundred times, your eye will develop naturally. Once you're able to really "see", you'll begin to take an interest in the paintings themselves and the artists. If you research them, you'll find out all sorts of things you didn't know before. Western paintings, especially, are often themed around history, the Greek myths, Christianity and so forth. Knowing even a bit about those topics will make the art far more compelling.

'So what I'm saying is: study aesthetics. Cooking is an integrated art. If you don't mobilise all five senses, you can't make good food.

'Ultimately, whether you grow or not depends on your will to improve. And it's easy to tell if someone has the will to improve or not. It's whether they take notes or not – that's it.'

Each lesson is precious to me. I've kept them close to my heart all these years.

Before I knew it, I'd written over ten pages.

'I think this'll do.' After putting the announcement and letter into a larger envelope, Ken-chan took his scales down from a shelf and weighed the packet. 'Over 100 grams, but under 150.' Then he opened an album filled with stamps, chose one for a happy occasion, and carefully pasted it on. 'OK, it's ready to go. All that's left is to slip it into the postbox outside the shop.'

I stood, straightened up, and bowed.

'Thank you so much for all your help with every last thing.'

Ken-chan waved me off, flustered. 'N-none of that, please. I feel like I may have meddled too much. I regret it if I was rude so do forgive me if I offended you.' Then he bowed deeply and it was my turn to be flustered.

Ken-chan saw me out, and I posted the letter and announcement with him looking on.

Memo Pads

'I wonder if this is OK . . . Was it the right thing to do?'

'I'm sure it'll be fine.' His voice sounded encouraging to my ears.

I nodded, took the Rhodia out of my pocket, and crossed off the remaining line, '*Send an announcement to Taisho, too.*'

* * *

One day in the busy month of December, the manager of Shihodo, Ken Takarada, was sweeping the pavement in front of the shop. It seemed he had a little more free time after wrapping up the orders for his corporate clients.

Along came the sushi chef Gin Fuda. Ken immediately greeted him.

'Good morning!'

'Hey, morning!'

Gin handed Ken a paper bag.

'I wanted you to try my *chirashizushi*, so I made some for you.'

Gin's place was an *omakase*-only high-end restaurant that cost upwards of 30,000 yen a head.

'Is it really OK for me to have this?!' Ken asked timidly as he took the bag, and Gin responded with a big smile.

'Of course, Ken-chan. I wanted to give you a little thank-you.'

'A thank-you?'

Gin scratched his head self-consciously and said, 'Yesterday, Taisho came to my restaurant.'

'Oh, really?'

'Yeah, really. Pretty early, too.'

'So how did it go?'

Gin laughed and said, 'Well, I open at six, but at a little before five I noticed someone walking back and forth out front. When I went out to take a look, it was the taisho. My mind went completely blank. "I-It's been quite a while," I said with a bow and he replied in the same old voice, "I'm sure you need a reservation to eat here, but do you think you might be able to squeeze me in?" I was done with prep, and I didn't have any reservations till seven, so I had him come right in.'

Just listening to the story must have been making Ken nervous. He swallowed hard. 'And? And?'

'When we went inside, he took the seat closest to the door and said, "I'll have sushi for one. And to drink, tea, please." I set out the tea and a hand towel immediately and began making the sushi. Usually I prepared a course, so there were appetisers, sashimi and other little dishes, and I could pair things with drinks . . . I was so nervous, wondering if I would really be able to impress him with just the sushi, but all I could do was believe in myself.'

'So how did he react?'

'That's the thing, no matter what I served, he didn't say a word – he just ate in total silence. I was scared to death. Well, every now and then he nodded and maybe said, "Aha", I guess. But then he even got out his Rhodia and took some notes. And of course, I had no idea what he was writing. I was worried sick.'

Ken nodded and said, 'I'm kind of terrified to hear what happened next.'

'I serve the sushi brushed with soy or other sauces, or topped with salt and *sudachi*, or whatnot, so customers can eat it as it is, but he was so fast. He ate so fast! The moment I said, "Tuna" or "Sea urchin" and set it on the board, his hand would flick out to snatch it and he'd pop it in his mouth. He'd chew slowly before swallowing, rinse with some tea, and then look at me as if to say, "Next!" All notion of pace went out of the window!'

Memo Pads

'Th-then what happened?'

'The last item to go out is a roll wrapped in seaweed. I don't think it took him even thirty minutes to eat eleven pieces of nigiri sushi plus that roll. Well, from my perspective, pressing each piece of sushi together, it was over in no time, but also felt like forever . . . I'm not really sure.'

Gin crossed his arms and fell silent. Ken watched his face intently.

'When I gave him a fresh cup of tea, he took maybe one sip and then stood up. He politely pushed his chair in, looked me straight in the eye, and said, "I learned a lot." He stood up straighter and bowed. Then he said, "It was delicious." I felt like I had to say something, but I couldn't think of anything at all. Finally I managed a "Thank you."'

'. . . Phew,' Ken couldn't help but murmur.

'Then he took a congratulatory envelope out of his jacket pocket and dropped it casually on the counter. "Just an expression of my feelings," he said. "You've worked hard." Then he was gone.'

Gin uncrossed his arms and bowed. 'It's all thanks to you, Ken-chan. I truly appreciate everything you've done for me.'

'Surely not "all", but I'm glad I was able to be of service.'

'I wonder if I can take advantage of your kindness again. Is the desk on the first floor open? I'd like to write Taisho a thank-you note for visiting the restaurant. And if it's not too much trouble, I'd like you to pick the stationery.'

'I'd be happy to,' Ken answered, opening the shop's glass door to invite Gin inside.

In one corner of Ginza, the venerable old stationery shop, Shihodo. This day, too, it seemed liable to be busy with regulars attracted by the personality of manager Ken Takarada.